JAMIE ✦ SMART'S

FLEMBER

THE POWER OF THE WILDENING

David Fickling Books

31 Beaumont Street
Oxford OX1 2NP, UK

FLEMBER: The Power of the Wildening
is a
DAVID FICKLING BOOK

First published in Great Britain in 2022 by
David Fickling Books,
31 Beaumont Street,
Oxford, OX1 2NP

978-1-78845-259-5

5 7 9 10 8 6 4

Papers used by David Fickling Books are from well-
managed forests and other responsible sources.

DAVID FICKLING BOOKS Reg. No. 8340307

A CIP catalogue record for this book is
available from the British Library.

Typeset by Falcon Oast Graphic Art Ltd, Tenterden, Kent

Printed and bound in Great Britain by Clays, Ltd, Elcograf S.p.A

Where there is no light, darkness grows.

FLEMBER

THE MYSTERIOUS, MAGICAL POWER THAT FLOWS THROUGH ALL LIVING THINGS!

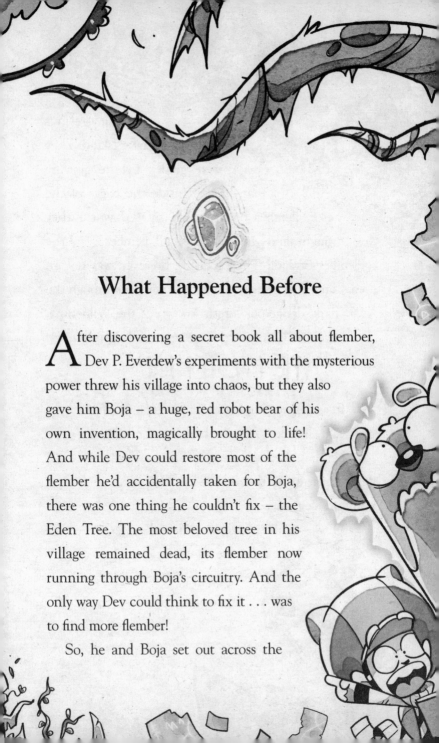

What Happened Before

After discovering a secret book all about flember, Dev P. Everdew's experiments with the mysterious power threw his village into chaos, but they also gave him Boja – a huge, red robot bear of his own invention, magically brought to life! And while Dev could restore most of the flember he'd accidentally taken for Boja, there was one thing he couldn't fix – the Eden Tree. The most beloved tree in his village remained dead, its flember now running through Boja's circuitry. And the only way Dev could think to fix it . . . was to find more flember!

So, he and Boja set out across the

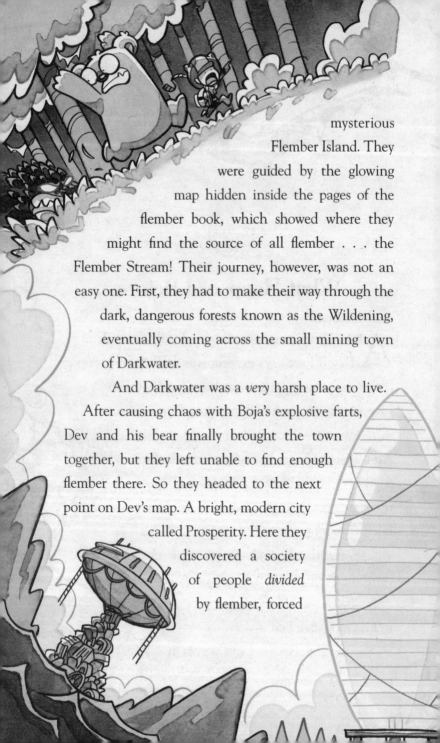

mysterious
Flember Island. They
were guided by the glowing
map hidden inside the pages of the
flember book, which showed where they
might find the source of all flember . . . the
Flember Stream! Their journey, however, was not an
easy one. First, they had to make their way through the
dark, dangerous forests known as the Wildening,
eventually coming across the small mining town
of Darkwater.

And Darkwater was a *very* harsh place to live.
After causing chaos with Boja's explosive farts,
Dev and his bear finally brought the town
together, but they left unable to find enough
flember there. So they headed to the next
point on Dev's map. A bright, modern city
called Prosperity. Here they
discovered a society
of people *divided*
by flember, forced

to fight amongst themselves for a chance at equality.

But Dev, Boja and Dev's brother, Santoro, managed to defeat Prosperity's extraordinary flember-fuelled technologies and help make it a fairer place to live.

As a reward, Boja was permitted to take a little extra flember, just enough to revive the Eden Tree. Dev also learnt that it was Dev and Santoro's father, Bartleby, who wrote the flember book!

With this revelation fresh in their minds, along with an awful lot of questions, Dev and Boja are now keen to head back through the Wildening.

To make their way home.

To heal the Eden Tree and restore the balance of flember once and for all.

1

The Journey Home

Santoro hacked through another thick clump of leaves with his sword.

'Dev, be serious for a moment,' he puffed, wiping the sweat from his forehead. 'Do you really think that your armour's going to protect you out *here*?'

Dev stumbled out from behind his brother, skidding slightly in the mossy mud. He picked at the armour he was wearing. It did look a little cobbled together since he had, literally, cobbled his broken armour back together. He'd hammered out the dents, replaced the flemberthyst crystals, then strung it all around his arms and legs with thin lengths of blackrock cord.

But still, he beamed proudly. 'I fixed it up as best I

could,' he replied, rapping his knuckles against his chest. The chestplate slipped from its buckles and FLOMP-ed down into the mud. Dev sheepishly picked it up and wedged it back into place.

Santoro frowned. He gripped his brother tightly by the crumpled shoulder guards. 'Dev, it's dangerous out here,' he whispered. 'Your inventions and your . . . your *fix-ups* won't keep you safe for long. You could have chosen proper armour from Prosperity, well-made armour, like *mine* . . .' Santoro took a deep breath. His fine, smart, flemberthyst-studded armour glistened magnificently in the early morning sunlight. 'But you didn't. So, instead, if we're going to survive in the Wildening, then I think maybe I should teach you how to defend yourself.'

'Fighting?' Dev shivered at the thought of it. 'Oh, no, that's your thing, Santoro, that's not for me. I use my head; I come up with *ideas*! I can invent anything with the help of my Tinkering Helmet!'

He cheerfully tugged on the chinstraps of his helmet. The two cat ears slid apart, and a cluster of broken, spindly metal rods unfolded, a fizzing lightbulb plink-plink-plinking between them.

Sparks flew.

Water trickled.

Something banged.

Santoro sighed loudly.

'Oh, I meant to fix that,' Dev muttered. Then a broad smile spread across his face. 'Anyway, we'll always be safe, as long as we have BOJA with us!'

He turned, hoping to see the big red bear behind them.

But there was no one there.

'Boja?' Dev called out hopefully. He peered through the rustling leaves, the winding bracken, the hefty, moss-spattered tree trunks.

His heart pounded a little faster.

'Boja?' he called again. 'BOJA, WHERE ARE—'

'HWU-U-U-U-U-URPPPPP!' something belched out from the shadows. A waft of smells floated across the Wildening around them, smells so sweet, so sugary, they made Dev's eyes twitch.

Then a huge, lumbering shape staggered out.

It glowed, and crackled, and sparkled with flember.

'Soh-rry.' Boja giggled, lifting a paw to wipe the trail of foody-spit from his mouth. In his other arm he carried the most precious of cargoes; an array of cakes he had grabbed before they left Prosperity. He scooped another splodge of glittery cream into his mouth and let out another joyful belch.

His flember glowed a little brighter.

'Boja . . . could . . . you . . . *focus*?' Santoro huffed, poking Boja in the belly on every word. 'We all need to be alert. Especially you. With all your wooshy, sparkly new powers,' – Santoro mimed the swish of Boja's flember gauntlets – 'we're going to need you when things get difficult.'

Dev plucked a chilli-frosted doughnut from Boja's pile and gleefully took a few chomps out of it. 'Andsch youff gotsch a lot more flember now,' he spluttered between chews before gulping a mouthful down. 'All the extra you took from Prosperity. You need to *protect* that flember until we can get you back to Eden!'

'O-K,' Boja mumbled, sadly.

'Don't worry, we'll be home before you know it.' Dev smiled. He popped the last clump of doughnut into his mouth, hauled the backpack from his shoulders, undid the buckles, reached inside, and pulled out the flember book. Dev spread the pages out, and gazed in delight at

9

the hidden map now glowing across them.

'Dad's *book* will lead us there.'

'I'm still not sure Dad wrote that book,' Santoro sighed, hacking at more leaves with his sword.

'But . . . but Santoro, our dad was the *Second Pioneer*! The one who discovered all of Flember Island's secrets!' Dev exclaimed. 'When we get home we'll ask Mum. She'll tell us it's true. She'll tell us *all* about him.'

Suddenly he noticed a clump of weird, pillowy pink flowers. 'I recognize these,' he muttered, flipping to the back of the flember book to a collection of slightly cleaner looking pages. 'Brianne let me take some of Dad's notes from Prosperity, where he had been sketching all the weird stuff that grows in the Wildening . . .

FIZZLEPLOPS!' he cried at the page he was looking for.
'These flowers are called *fizzleplops*!'

Dev crouched down, and gently poked the petals.

'Oh, no, hang on, it says I *shouldn't* poke it.'

Suddenly – with a loud F-Z-Z-Z-Z! – the fizzleplop
exploded into a plume of pink sparkles. Dev coughed,
and he spluttered, and then, with an almost audible
DING, an idea bubbled up into his brain.

'Maybe we could wrap the fizzleplops up, enclose them
in some kind of casing . . .' He closed his book, slid it into
his backpack, then slowly, carefully, plucked a fizzleplop
up by its stalk. Then he wrapped a thick green leaf around
it. 'So if we ever lose sight of each other, we can fire them
into the sky! Like FLARES! FIZZING FLARES!'

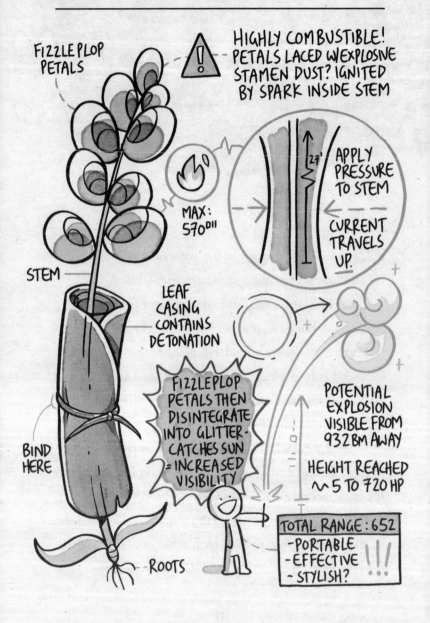

He leant down to pick another, only for it to suddenly F-Z-Z-Z-Z-Z in Dev's hands.

'ARGH!' Dev yelped in surprise, dropping it into the other fizzleplops, which WOOSH-ed and FRRRPPP-ed into a huge bubbling explosion of pink lights. Dev stumbled backwards. His boots slipped from beneath him. With a muffled 'OOF!' he slammed into Boja's soft belly which, in turn, knocked Boja off his balance. Cream-frosted nipperknockles, glazed chiplets, and half a pound of whipped clophooves flew from Boja's arms, sailing up into the air before falling SPLAT! SPLOT! SPLOTCH! down on to the ground.

Dev was a little shaken, but Boja was *distraught*.

'CAKES!' the bear yelped, throwing himself on to all fours as his huge pink tongue slid along the ground. It slurped up dollops of cream and sponge, and a good clump of dirt and twigs along with it, as he zigzagged a trail into the taller grass.

'Boja, be careful,' Santoro shouted.

'MY BREAKFASCHT!' Boja chomped, spotting another of his escaped cakes. A glazed chiplet thoroughly splatted into the soil. With a loud SLURP his tongue scooped it, and a large wodge of mud, up into his mouth.

He chewed with noisy glee.

And then he stopped, his cheeks still bulging.

'Whasschat?' he belched.

Dev froze too. He could hear it.

Something was growling.

He hoped at first it might be Boja's belly, hungry for a second round of mud-soaked cakes, but then he saw movement through the tall grass. It looked like a shadow. The jagged black spikes of its back slinked up and down. Its head lifted, its muzzle bunched into a snarl, its lips quivered open to reveal two rows of sharp, pointed teeth.

Its red, glowing eyes were trained upon Boja.

'A dark wolf!' Dev whispered. His blood ran cold. He could feel the scratches upon his arm, the bite marks, start to throb.

'There'll be another,' Santoro hissed. His armour was already lighting up, its flemberthysts blazing as he clutched his sword in both hands. 'There's always more than one.'

As if summoned, another dark wolf emerged from between the trees. It flanked Boja from the other side. Boja, now realizing he was surrounded, gulped down his muddy chiplet. Then his face scrunched into a look of defiance. The flember crackling across his fur started to blaze. It writhed around him in wide glowing arcs, before snaking down his arms, circling around his fists like a pair of huge sparkling gauntlets.

Boja looked fierce.

He looked incredible.

'Two dark wolves will be no match for us this time!' Dev said, only to catch sight of more movement. More dark, cruel, jagged, shapes slinking through the long grass. One after the other, after the other.

'A whole pack of them, though,' Santoro snarled, watching the dark wolves circle Boja as if he were a cream-frosted nipperknockle. 'That could be more difficult.'

2

Decoy

Dev's arm throbbed down into the bones. His head started to swim. His legs trembled. The dark wolves did this to him. Somehow, being near them always made him feel *weaker*.

Boja, however, wasn't wasting a second.

'HWOOOOOARGHHH!' he roared, swinging his bright, sparkling gauntlets back before slamming them down hard into the ground. Everything shook. The wolves scattered. Then they regrouped. Behind him. Around him. Crouched low beneath the long grass. Only the jagged spines along their backs gave them away.

Dev steadied himself. Took a deep breath. Lifted his head. Gradually, his makeshift flember armour started to light up. He took one step, then another, and then, suddenly, in a blaze of crackling flember, he was speeding towards the nearest wolf. It turned, opening its jaws wide and chomped onto his forearm. Its jagged black teeth buckled the protective plates of his armour but didn't pierce it. Dev wrenched his arm out, barging his whole weight against the wolf before staggering, flemberthysts blazing, towards the next.

'MINE!' Santoro had already marked this wolf. He skidded past Dev, then lunged with his sword.

CHI-I-I-I-INGGG! It threw out sparks from the wolf's neck, carving barely a scratch against its thick black skin.

Dev and Santoro both stared at each other in disbelief.

'It's like they're made of *blackrock*,' Dev cried. 'And blackrock's too strong! Too solid to break! Even flember can't pass through it!'

Santoro let out an exasperated gasp. 'Then how do we fight them, Dev? How do we BEAT them?'

'*We* can't. But maybe BOJA can! BOJA! LIGHT THEM UP!'

'HWO-O-O-O-A-A-R-GHHHH!' Boja roared, even louder than before. The crackles of flember dancing across his fur started to pulse brighter, bigger, before suddenly exploding in a blinding light. It flung a number of dark wolves into the sky. DOOMPF! They fell back into the long grass like hailstones. DOOMPF! DOOMPF! DOOMPF!

Boja's eyes scrunched into a squint. His glistening teeth ground together. His fur prickled up on end.

'MY cakes,' he growled, scooping one more chiplet from the ground and defiantly cramming it into his mouth.

The wolves, however, weren't scared of him. If anything, they only looked more determined. Again they raced forwards, weaving between Boja's glowing gauntlets, defying his bright, crackling flember as they threw themselves against him. They clung, and they crawled

over his body like bumbleflies across a stinky piece of meat.

'BOJA, WAIT THERE!' Dev yelled, as he spun on his heels and ran, not towards the bear, but out from the long grass, up on to the rockier ground, towards the protruding clump of pink fizzleplop flowers. With increasing urgency he grasped a fistful of stalks and yanked them out. The fizzleplops instantly burst into a plume of fizzing, sparkling lights around him.

Then he held them out towards the wolves.

'Hey! Wolves! If you really want to take a bite out of anyone, I'm a far easier target! My armour's falling apart, you could chew through it in no time!'

The wolves all looked round, their red eyes glaring at Dev.

'Dev, what are you doing?' Santoro yelled, his sword clamped between a dark wolf's jaws.

Dev's stomach gurgled.

'I'm not entirely sure,' he whimpered. 'Trying to save Boja?'

Suddenly the wolves leapt from Boja's back. They dived into the long grass, streamed past the swing of Santoro's sword, and sped towards Dev.

Dev let out a yelp so high-pitched even he couldn't hear it.

'Run,' he muttered to himself, as if willing his feet to start moving. 'Run run run run RUN!'

What remained of his flember armour started to crackle once again. Then, with a panicked squawk, Dev was gone. Racing as fast as his legs would carry him through a corridor of tall trees, while a trail of pink sparkling smoke drifted out behind him. Above the sounds of his own heartbeat pounding in his ears, he could still hear the wolves. He could hear their paws pounding against the ground. Their snaps. Their howls. Their snarls gurgling in their throats.

'Faster!' Dev winced, his last few flemberthysts already shining at their brightest. 'Faster-r-r-r!'

His legs powered him through the Wildening at speeds he didn't know he was capable of. Branches whipped against his face. The ground squelched beneath his feet. Then, suddenly, it slipped away completely. Dev found himself skidding down a steep gravel slope, his armour crumpling and tearing as he bounced from one sharp rock to another. He turned his head to see that the dark wolves, too, were hurtling down the slope. Their legs scrambled helplessly as they growled and yelped, slamming against the rocks, rolling between the trees. One by one they disappeared. Falling down into sunken hollows and crevices, slipping between the gaps in the Wildening.

By the time Dev reached flatter
ground his armour was in tatters
– just a few plates remained. But
he didn't slow down. He kept
running across the gravel,
as far as he could
possibly go.

All the way to the very edge of a cliff, with a wide,
pale sky above him, and only tree tops far, far below.

He skidded to a halt. A cold wind hit sharply inside
his lungs as he bowed, struggling to catch his breath.
'I can't . . .' he gasped. His flember armour flickered.
'I can't . . . run any more.' Slowly, achingly, he turned
around. He dropped the smouldering fizzleplops. His
body felt drained now, with barely a drop of strength left
in it.

But he made himself stand tall, defiant.

Fists clenched.

Heart pounding.

'Maybe Santoro's right,' he whispered under his breath. 'Maybe I will have to *fight* my way out of this one.'

He dug his heel into the cliff edge. His eyes frantically scanned the slope, searching for any dark wolves that might still be following him, hiding amongst the trees, slinking behind the rocks. Soon, however, he realized there were none. Whether they had been lost to the Wildening, or given up the chase, one way or another he had lost them.

He unclenched his fists.

Took a deep breath.

He was about to start the long walk back, when he caught the sound of something on the wind. Not the snarling of a dark wolf, but something more . . . musical. A strange, disjointed melody. A clatter of thumps and screeches. At first it was faint, but as he looked around to see where it was coming from it grew louder. And louder. And LOUDER. Suddenly the noise was all around him. It pounded through the ground. It rattled through his head. Dev clamped his hands over his ears. He swung around, disorientated, only to bump into something that hadn't been there before. He blinked to try and make sense of it. It was taller than him. Heavy looking. Dark. It wore a cloak of what looked like crumpled, dead leaves, that hung loosely over its crooked body.

Its head appeared to be an old, cracked skull, its long beak pointing down towards Dev as it stared at him through red, glowing eyes.

Dev scrambled back as far as he could, to the very edge of the cliff. He couldn't work out what this creature was. It looked like an animal, of sorts, but it made strange clicking noises as it moved.

'W . . . w . . . whatever you are, I just want to go home,' he stammered, his trembling hands gripping on to the rocks. 'I . . . I just want to get back to Eden.'

The creature tilted its head slightly, as if it was studying him. Then a mesh of long, thin tendrils rose out from beneath its cloak. They planted themselves into the grassy ground between Dev's boots, flember crackling loudly as it swarmed up from the now dying grass, and into the creature's body.

An eerie red glow appeared all around it.

'You're stealing flember from the *ground*,' Dev whispered, amazed.

Suddenly, the creature lurched towards him.

Dev shrieked, scuttling back, but there was nowhere to go. His boots slipped. The cliff edge crumbled beneath him. With his heart in his mouth Dev's whole body toppled backwards, before tumbling silently down, down, all the way down into the valley below.

3

What Else is Here?

Dev fell for some distance, he skidded against the steep sides of the cliff before bouncing across its boulders with a sickening array of thuds and crunches.

'OW! YOW!' he yelped. 'OW-W-W!'

The last few pieces of his armour took the brunt. Its flemberthysts smashed, its protective limbs splintered away. It was all but gone by the time Dev hit solid ground again and rolled, exhausted, across a stretch of grass.

He lay there for a little while, and waited for his brain to stop spinning inside his head. Then he took a deep breath, heaved himself up with his arms, and pulled away the last few broken bits of armour from his body. 'Well, it kept me safe for a *while*,' he muttered, before glancing, nervously, up towards the clifftop.

Whatever that creature was, he couldn't see it any more.

Nor could he hear the strange music.

'At least I led the dark wolves away from Santoro and Boja,' Dev sighed with relief. He staggered on to his feet and scanned for a foothold in the cliff face. 'But I need to get back to them. They won't know where I am!'

Then he paused.

'Hang on, *I* don't know where I am.' He gulped.

He stepped back on to the grass. The clouds had greyed, and drizzle now floated in the air, but there was still plenty of colour in this corner of the Wildening. The trees were peppered with bright red mushrooms. The rocks splattered with plump green moss. And there were flowers, huge clumps of flowers – orange pipplelilies, yellow fissletails . . .

He hurried over to a spindletree, knelt down amongst its tangled roots and searched eagerly. 'If I could find some fizzleplops, I could make more flares,' he puffed.

'Then I could use them to show Santoro and Boja just where I am!'

Then his fingers touched something furry.

He looked up.

Whatever he was looking at rustled back at him.

'YARGHHH!' Dev cried, scooting away. 'Get away from me! GET AWAY!'

'POCKLE!' The creature's voice sounded younger than Dev was expecting. Then it giggled.

Still, he picked up a stick and held it out, trembling, as the creature slowly stepped out from the trees and into the cold, grey daylight.

'Pockle,' it chuckled again.

Dev could see it more clearly now. Half-buried inside a matted tangle of hair, leaves, fur and mud, was the face of a little girl.

'You're . . . you're human?' he gasped, as she pattered a few steps closer. She didn't seem able to hear him, until she lifted the matted tangle away from her ears.

'I was HIDING!'

Her cheeks pinched into an excited, gap-toothed smile. Her eyes glistened with excitement.

Dev carefully took to his feet. 'Hiding . . . from the Wildening?'

'Hiding from *you*!' she cried with delight. 'But you found me! Now *you* go and hide!'

Without waiting for a response she put her hands over her eyes and started counting. 'One . . . two . . . three . . . go as far as you like.' She giggled again. 'I'll still find you!'

Dev slow-w-w-wly placed his stick on the ground. He was a little unsure what to make of all this. His body had only just stopped shaking after his fall, and now this little girl wanted to play hide and seek with him . . . in the *Wildening*?

'What . . . what's your name?' he asked.

'I told you! Pockle!' the girl replied, then returned to her counting. 'Eight . . . nine . . . ten-n-n-n.' She sneaked one eye open from between her fingers. 'You're not HIDING!'

Dev cleared his throat, then crouched down in front of her. 'Pockle, my name's Dev,' he said. 'I've lost my brother and my bear. There are monsters out here, didn't you know that? Really *scary* monsters. It's not safe!'

'The camp is safe!' Pockle replied.

'Camp? Do you live nearby?'

Pockle lowered her hands. She nodded proudly, then gripped her muddy little fingers around Dev's hands. 'I'll SHOW you!' she said, pulling him with a surprisingly strong yank.

'W-w-well, OK!' Dev stuttered nervously, following the strange, rustling, humming little girl into the shadow of the trees. 'And we'll look out for each other. In case anything *attacks*.'

'Oh, we'll be fine,' Pockle yelled back. 'I have Gollup to keep me safe!'

'Goll-up?'

Suddenly he noticed the lump of mud on top of Pockle's head start to move. Something was uncurling from underneath. It was . . . yawning. It was . . .

Glowing!

'Gollup!' it burped, sleepily.

Dev's mouth flapped open in astonishment. 'Pockle, w-w-what is . . . *that?*'

Pockle stopped. She reached up, took the strange glistening slug in her hands, and carefully handed it over to Dev.

It felt squishy. Sticky. A little slimy. It blinked at him through two shining eyes. 'He already told you. His name is Gollup,' she grinned. 'If you're scared, he can keep you safe too.'

4

The Camp

'It's like he's *made* of flember,' Dev gasped, carrying Gollup the slug out in front of him as if he were carrying the most precious jewel on the island. 'I can *feel* the flember coming off him. And I can see every vein, every heartbeat glowing through his body!'

Gollup let out a contented purr.

'He PURRS too!' Dev squeaked. 'I've never seen anything *like* it!'

Pockle shared another great big smile with Dev. 'I summoned Gollup all by myself,' she proudly declared.

'Summoned? What do you mean?'

Pockle reached into her muddy, rustly camouflage, and pulled out what looked like a rattle. 'I used my *totem*,' she chirped, waving it around. 'I summoned a flember slug from the ground. I did it on my first try too. Elder Nakobe was VERY impressed!'

If anything, this answered none of Dev's questions, and only gave him a whole lot more. He'd barely had a chance to open his mouth, however, when Pockle stopped sharply in front of him.

'Camp!' she announced.

The camp, it appeared, was a rather small one. It sat in a clearing of trees, a few small wooden huts surrounded by a rickety wooden fence, hardly well protected from all the horrors of the Wildening. But still, Pockle was excited to be back. She took Gollup from Dev's hands, plopped him back on top of her head, rustled a few leaves over him, and skipped cheerfully through the open gate.

Dev followed. 'You live . . . here?' he asked, as he walked between the huts. They were old, shabby, and they seemed to be held together by rope, their holes patched up with dollops of dry mud. Broken pieces of wood lay scattered around: wheels, barrels, bits of a chair. Racks covered with dried flowers and plants had been propped against each other. Bowls lined the path. Dev crouched down to see a pink paste smeared inside them.

'Fizzleplops!' he exclaimed, picking out a few crinkled fizzleplop petals. 'Dried, and then crushed, and somehow they didn't explode! Could I use a little bit of this, Pockle?'

Pockle shrugged cheerfully, before ducking inside one of the huts.

Taking that as a yes, Dev carefully spooned out a small dollop of the paste and smeared it inside a leaf. He pinched it together. Held it above his head. Then he started shaking it. The fizzleplop flare started to sputter, bang, and then FOOOSH, it exploded, sending a cloud of pink dust crackling and fizzing up into the trees.

'It might just be bright enough for Santoro or Boja to see,' Dev muttered hopefully. 'It might be enough for them to find me!'

Suddenly, by the flickering light of the fizzleplop flare, Dev saw something out in the shadows. His pulse quickened.

'They're not here!' Pockle whined, running out from the hut. 'Elder Nakobe, she's not—'

Dev clamped a hand around her mouth, and then, as Gollup started to yawn, another hand around his.

'Shhhh,' Dev whispered. His wide eyes fixed beyond the fence. 'I think the dark wolves might have followed us here!'

Before he could reach for another dollop of fizzleplop paste, however, two figures lunged out from between the trees. They leapt over the fence in a holler of noises. Not wolves, but children. The boy wore what looked like a dingo skull on his head, with feathers poking out of it, and a body of furs that made him look even stockier than he already was. The girl running behind was taller and slimmer, with antlers poking out from either side of her pointed hat. While the boy angrily wielded what looked like a club, she held out a bow, slipping loose an arrow towards Dev without any warning.

'INTRUDER!' she yelled. The arrow THUNK-ed into a hut wall beside Dev, then exploded in a crackle of pink lights. Dev barely had time to react before the boy had reached into his pocket and flung out what looked like neatly wrapped pebbles, which WHIZZ-ed and BANG-ed in front of Dev's boots.

'I call this my hitting stick,' the boy declared, swinging the tip of his club under Dev's nose. 'And I might just have to use it, because you're on SACRED TRAINING GROUND, reserved for children of the Wildening only!'

The girl nocked another arrow in her bow. 'Pockle! Step away from the weird boy!'

Pockle giggled.

Dev pushed the boy's hitting stick from under his nostrils. 'I'm . . . I'm not weird,' he protested. 'And I'm not an intruder, either!'

'He's my friend!' Pockle said.

'I . . . I found her in the Wildening,' Dev added.

'I found YOU!'

A noise interrupted them. Dev could hear a word, repeated over and over again, getting louder as it got closer. Trees creaked and crashed. Footsteps pounded. The ground shook. The children of the Wildening tensed up in fear until whatever had been causing the commotion suddenly burst into view.

'BREAKFAST!' Boja boomed, before tripping over the fence and slamming face-first on to the ground. Then he was up again, a huge goofy grin still plastered across his mouth as he barrelled through the camp. Dev barely stood a chance. Before he'd even said the B of 'BOJA!' the great big bear rolled him up into a great big furry hug. Then CRUNCH! Boja slumped against one of the huts, his huge bum knocking it off its legs, and on to its side.

Even though Dev was now smothered in red fur, in his ears, up his nose, his heart pounded with joy.

'Bfscha, you schfound me!' Dev coughed through a mouthful of belly fluff. Then he leant back, patting the bear's fur, searching for bites or scratches. 'But are you hurt? The wolves, did they come back for you?'

'Wolves all gone! Went with you!' Boja cheered, before sque-e-e-ezing Dev even tighter. 'Then we saw FLARE. Then I got HUNGRY!' He noticed a bowl filled with pink paste, which he dipped his finger into, and then sucked on. A crackle of small explosions spilled out of his mouth.

'A . . . A MONSTER!' The boy with the hitting stick gibbered frantically. 'And it's inside our camp!' Then, with all the bravery he could muster, he poked his stick hard into Boja's bum cheek. Boja released Dev from the hug, as he stood, turning to face the boy with the biggest, meanest, most scowling face he could muster.

The boy backed away, terrified, unable to look away from all the little pink lights exploding across Boja's tongue.

'Boja doesn't like being called a monster,' Santoro said, as the boy bumped up against him. The blade of Santoro's drawn sword glinted in the boy's eyes. 'And he *definitely* doesn't like being poked in the bottom.'

'You leave my brother alone!' The trembling girl switched her drawn arrow between Boja and Santoro, unsure which of them to aim at. 'We're highly trained! Our . . . our flember skills are unmatched!'

'PENA!' came a far older, croakier voice.

Instantly the girl lowered her bow.

'BAGBY!'

The boy sheepishly hid the hitting stick behind his back. Both of them stood to one side, as Dev watched a rather round, elderly woman shuffle in through the front gate. She wore a tall hat shaped like a biscuit tin, with flaps down either side of her painted face. Her many,

many different cloaks dragged behind her, as she steadied herself on an old staff topped by a lantern. On her back she carried what looked like a set of shelves. They heaved with all manner of collected items. Cups, pans, plants, jars, cactuses. All clinking and clanking as she took every slow, careful step.

She looked tired.

She looked annoyed.

'*Jijonjay reckiso funsch*,' she muttered grumpily. 'We do not . . . *attack* . . . our guests.'

5
A New Plan

'An *Oracle*!' Dev gasped. He stepped towards the elderly lady, marvelling at the painted blue dots around her eyes. 'The markings . . . on your face, I've seen them before. You're an Oracle, just like the one I met at the very top of Prosperity's Spire!'

The elderly lady shook her head.

'Oracle? . . . My *sister*!' she snorted.

'Oh!' Dev stumbled to find his next words.

'I . . . I'm sorry.

I just assumed . . .' He cleared his throat and nervously shuffled his feet. 'I should tell you what happened to her. I was there, you see, and she . . . well, she sort of . . . *disappeared* into the Flember Stream.'

A thin finger and thumb reached up and clamped Dev's lips shut. 'I know.' The woman nodded, politely. But she wasn't listening to him any more. Instead she was staring at Boja. The many, many wrinkles across her face converged into a huge smile. Slowly, with all her shelves clanging behind her, she shuffled towards him, palms out as if she planned to ruffle his big red cheeks. Then she paused, reached into one of the many holdalls strapped around her waist, and pulled out a bunch of bright yellow grapes.

Boja's nostrils widened.

NIFF! NIFF NIFF!

The little pink tip of his tongue poked out, as though he was about to delicately lick the dew off the grape nearest to him. Then, in an instant, he opened his mouth wide and CHOMPED the entire bunch in one go.

'Breakfascht.' He chewed blissfully.

The woman watched in delight as Boja's flember skipped across his fur. It snaked, and crackled, and pulsed with every bite. Then she started clapping, pointing at Boja as if he was dancing a ridiculous little dance.

Which he then started to do.

'Elder Nakobe!' Bagby puffed out his chest and thumped the ground with his hitting stick. 'We tried to keep the camp safe while you were gone.' He reached a hand beneath his cloak, and pulled out a handful more pebbles from inside. 'I used the pink flower paste to make *bangers*, to scare away intruders.'

Pena stood as alert as her brother. 'I made exploding arrows.' She ran a finger along the shaft of her arrow, grinning as little pink sparks danced against the palm of her hand. 'I infused the wood with paste, so—'

But Elder Nakobe was not impressed with either of them. 'FENCE!' She shouted, pointing her long staff towards the perimeter of the camp. *'Ninakay POCKLE.'*

Both Bagby and Pena stared sheepishly at the ground.

'We . . . we only left the camp for a bit!' Pena mumbled.

'Fine! We went into the Wildening!' Bagby declared. 'But we did it to practise our flember! We were working on our summoning! You've not shown us how to do it yet so we, well, we wanted to try it out!'

'POCKLE!' Elder Nakobe's frown looked grumpier than Bagby's.

44

'Pockle's good at summoning already,' Pena grumbled. 'Anyway, she was asleep when we left. How were we to know she'd creep out too?'

'I didn't creep, I hid!' Pockle peered out from behind Boja, her hands clinging tightly on to his fur. Upon her head, the ever-sleepy Gollup yawned. This, it seemed, was the first time Boja had noticed Gollup, if the high pitch of his SQUEAL was anything to go by. He leapt on the spot, spinning around and shaking his paws with uncontrollable excitement. Then, once his breathing had slowed down a little, he reached down, and gently allowed Gollup to crawl on to one of his fingers.

'Gollup,' Gollup burped, as Boja lifted him up closer to his wide, astonished eyes.

'Bohhhhh-ja,' Boja cooed. He watched in amazement as his flember danced through Gollup's body, lighting it up a little brighter. Gollup smiled. Then nuzzled against Boja's nose.

The rest of the camp watched in silence.

'Well, this has been nice.' Santoro sheathed his sword. 'But we really have to go.'

'Wait, what does *summoning* mean?' Dev interrupted. 'Pockle said she summoned Gollup. Bagby, Pena, you were both working on your summoning. How . . . how do you *summon* things?'

Bagby walked forwards, raising himself up on the tips of his toes until he was nearly the same height as Dev. He jutted his chin out defiantly. 'We've been sent out here to train. To learn the ways of flember!' He pulled out his own totem, much like Pockle's, and clenched his fist tight around its handle. 'We're going to become super powerful! If you think Pockle's glowing lump of snot is clever, you wait till *I* start summoning flember. You wait till I'm riding a glowing tiger, or a glowing elephant, or . . . or a whole DOHAN!'

'*Dohan rejonday.*' Elder Nakobe shook her head.

'*Dohan sind jiji!*' Bagby insisted, shaking his totem harder.

Pena rolled her eyes. 'We're not very good at summoning flember yet.' She sighed. She pulled out her totem, and waved it idly in front of her. 'We only just started our training. Elder Nakobe has us crushing fizzleplop flowers and making boiled bilderberry grape stew for dinner. She hasn't taught us any of the cool stuff yet.'

They both stared, longingly, at Elder Nakobe's staff.

Or rather, Dev realized, her *totem.*

He could feel an excitement churning inside his belly. 'Do you think you could teach me about summoning too, Elder Nakobe?' He beamed. 'I thought I knew a lot already, but I've never seen anything like Gollup before.'

'GOLLUP!' Gollup belched from Boja's fingers. Boja squealed again. He hopped from one foot to the other, utterly delighted at this new friend. 'GOH-LLUP!' he belched back, before gently lowering the little glowing slug back on to Pockle's head.

Then he hopped about a bit more, unable to stop applauding.

'Dev, we're not staying here,' Santoro said. 'We need to get home. *You* wanted to get Boja back to the Eden Tree.'

'And I do! And we will! But look at that little thing, that *Gollup*,' Dev whispered gleefully in Santoro's ear. 'Have you ever seen anything so . . . so *magical*? I have to find out more. I just have to!'

Before Santoro could huff, or puff, or even reply, Elder Nakobe had stepped between them. She gripped Dev's arm, and turned it towards her. 'Wildening already . . . *hurt* you.' she said, staring at the dark scratches on his right arm.

'It's fine,' Dev insisted, pulling his arm away before she could look too closely. 'It doesn't hurt, not unless I get too close to the dark wolves. Then I start to feel a bit unwell.'

'*Jonto riri sip sep*,' Elder Nakobe muttered.

Dev looked to Bagby and Pena for a translation.

'FIELD TRIP!' Bagby suddenly cheered, raising his fists in the air.

'FIELD TRI-I-I-I-IP!' Pena whooped.

'What . . . *what's* happening?' Dev asked, a little startled. 'Why are you both so excited?'

'Elder Nakobe says there's no way you can go through the Wildening alone.' Bagby beamed. 'She probably thinks it's too dangerous for you. Especially if you don't know the ways of flember, like we do.'

'Like we *will*,' Pena rolled her eyes again. 'One day. But for now, Elder Nakobe is going to guide you all back home.'

'And she can't trust us here alone.' Bagby grinned proudly, slipping his hitting stick down the back of his cloak. 'So we're all coming with you!'

Pockle let out an excited meep. Boja did too, still staring at the sleeping Gollup upon her head. Elder Nakobe sighed long, loudly enough for everyone to hear that she wasn't entirely happy with how things had worked out.

'Works for me.' Santoro nudged his brother. 'There's safety in numbers.'

Dev smiled. 'Me too,' he said. 'And maybe she can teach us how to summon flember on the way!'

6

Following the Trail

Elder Nakobe marched swiftly, purposefully, through the Wildening. Her shelves of pots and pans

TINK-CLONK-CLANG-ed merrily behind her. Dev followed closely, hovering around her, asking a hundred different questions, but not getting much in the way of a reply to any of them. Boja kept a few steps further back. Occasionally he would pluck more grapes from the trees and SLUR-R-R-RP them down, and each time he did, Santoro cringed a little more. The noises were making him look rather queasy.

Bagby and Pena held the rear. Bagby, for reasons best known to himself, kept sniffing the trees, while Pena walked proudly with her bow drawn, ready to defend the group at a moment's notice. Occasionally, Pockle popped out from behind a shrub. Every time she did Boja cheered,

mostly at the sight of a sleepy, glowing Gollup upon her head, which gave Pockle enough encouragement to run off and hide somewhere else.

The air was becoming warmer. The breeze smelt a little sweeter. Dev could see the late-morning sun creeping between the trees; trees which, for most of their time in the Wildening, had always felt menacing, looming over them like a constant threat. Now, however, he found them rather comforting. Orange and yellow tinged the tips of their green leaves. The first rusty colours of autumn were sneaking in. And with Elder Nakobe leading them back towards the southernmost mountain, back home to Eden, all thoughts of the dark wolves, even the terrifying creature with the loud music, started to fade from Dev's mind.

He hustled a little closer to Elder Nakobe. 'Can you see the future too?' he whispered sheepishly. 'The Oracle . . . she could tap into the Flember Stream! She could read it like a book. She knew everything that was happening, and everything that was *about* to happen!'

Elder Nakobe stopped. She turned. Chuckled. 'Oracle . . . *very* special.' She smiled. 'Told me . . . you were on your way.'

The fine hairs on Dev's neck bristled. 'W-wait, how . . . how did she tell you that?' he stammered.

Elder Nakobe tilted her head, listening to the breeze. Dev listened too, as if he might hear something, but all he could hear was the slurping, chomping and belching – and the gentle continual farting – of the big red bear beside him.

'Oracle is . . . *sinjiki te* . . . *at one* with Flember Stream. With island.' Elder Nakobe held her totem upside down, resting its lantern against the ground.

'We are all . . .' she whispered, '*connected.*'

A light started to glow inside the lantern. A beautiful, sparkling, blue light which drifted out, before sinking gently into the leaf-covered mud. Dev watched in amazement as the ground beneath his boots started to glisten. Tiny pinpricks of light danced beneath the soil. Light which started to stretch, and curl, and tangle between the trees like a huge shimmering net.

'The tree roots,' Dev gasped. 'You're lighting up the tree roots . . . with flember!' He looked at his brother,

who was admiring the glow beneath his feet. He looked up at Boja, who was too busy eating grapes to notice what was going on. Then he stared, open-mouthed, back down at the roots, just as a line of tiny glowing mushrooms started to PLIP-PLIP-PLIPPP out of the ground, forming what looked like a thin path between the trees.

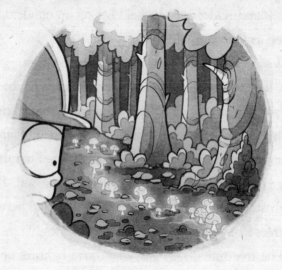

'Flember guides the way.' Elder Nakobe nodded.

Bagby, however, didn't seem quite as impressed. 'Oh, she does this sometimes, when she gets lost,' he snorted, standing beside Dev. 'It's amazing the first couple of times. She won't tell us how she does it though. She won't teach *us* how to summon.'

Elder Nakobe waddled along the trail of mushrooms. 'Bagby, Pena,' she called back. 'You will learn what you need . . . *shintojeh mep* . . . when you *need* it.'

Dev excitedly followed Elder Nakobe. 'When . . . when might I need to learn?' he asked, ducking beneath an archway of low-hanging branches. 'Because if you can teach me anything more about flember . . .'

His voice trailed off.

And the most fragrant smells hit his nose.

The mushrooms had led them into a wide open meadow. Brightly coloured flowers dotted the long grass; a sea of swaying reds, whites and yellows, all stretched out beneath an infinitely blue sky. Elder Nakobe strode between them, as Dev ran along behind her. He ran his fingers along the petals, savouring a calm he'd never expected to find in the Wildening.

Then he noticed the butterflies.

They fluttered around the glowing light from Nakobe's totem. Each of them sparkled, almost translucent in the sunlight, as flember glistened inside their delicate wings.

'These . . . these are creatures *made* of flember!' Dev gasped.

Elder Nakobe smiled. 'Flember *gives* . . .' she said, allowing one of the butterflies to land on her finger. '. . . if we . . . *hanjoh teh sepp* . . . if we know how to *ask*.'

She winked at Dev.

'I *teach* you how to ask.'

7

Summoning

'YEEEEEE!' Boja suddenly rushed past, flinging himself up into the sky as if he was diving into an enormous bowl of trifle. Then FLOOMPH! He landed, belly-first, in a brightly coloured plume of flowers, before rolling back and forth, flember crackling across his fur, as he squeaked, and honked, and giggled with delight.

'Is this still the way home?' Santoro walked through the flowers of the meadow, his hair flopping in the gentle breeze. He squinted towards the faint mountain in the distance. 'Is that . . . is that *Eden*?'

Dev excitedly gripped his brother by the arms. 'Santoro, Elder Nakobe's going to teach me,' he burbled. 'I think she's going to teach me flember summoning.

56

Whatever brought those butterflies to her,' he gestured to the butterflies hovering around Elder Nakobe's totem. 'She's going to teach ME how to do it!'

'SUMMONING?' Bagby roared as he stomped through the meadow. He waggled his own totem high above his head. 'Pena, come quick! Elder Nakobe's finally gonna show us how to do it!'

Pena ran after her brother. 'Oh I've been waiting for this! We're ready, Elder Nakobe, we're ready!'

Elder Nakobe looked around her, a little perturbed. 'Pockle?' she asked.

'POCKLE!' Pockle suddenly poked her head out from the thick carpet of flowers. Gollup dozed gently on her head. 'Aww, you found me,' she mumbled, before her eyes lit up again. 'COUNT TO TEN AND THEN COME LOOK!'

And with that Pockle and Gollup, were gone, still playing a game no one else was particularly joining in with.

'*Yopah-lay fen jens,*' Elder Nakobe announced. 'To summon flember, you will all need . . . totem.'

Bagby waggled his

proudly in front of him. Pena pulled hers out from her cloak, and clutched it keenly with both hands.

Then they both looked to Dev.

'I . . . I don't have one,' Dev's heart sank. 'Maybe if I could find Pockle she might lend me hers?'

Elder Nakobe shook her head. 'Wait,' she said. 'Bagby, Pena, go *first*.'

Bagby and Pena could barely contain their excitement. It took Elder Nakobe a few moments to calm them down, then she spoke slowly and carefully.

'*Roots*.' She closed her eyes, and held out her hands. 'As I showed you. *Giteh son ge ge*. Find the Flember Stream by the roots which lead us to it.'

Bagby was first to try, kneeling down and thumping his totem into the mud. He clenched his eyes shut. Then he strai-i-i-ined his face so tightly he went bobbleberry red and a fart slipped out of his back end, much to Boja's giggling delight.

But Bagby didn't laugh. Bagby was concentrating.

'Come ooonnn . . .' he pleaded. 'Gimme a Dohan, come OONN!'

Dev noticed something snuffle its way through the flowers. It was an animal, for sure, but it didn't glow like Gollup. It didn't sparkle like the flember butterflies.

It did, however, look a lot like a young wilderpig.

It smelt like a young wilderpig. It was chewing a selection of dillydaisies like a young wilderpig. And as it snuffled, then screeched, then bounded towards Bagby, leaping up against him and dragging its slimy wet tongue across his entire face, finally he realized what it was too.

'WILDERPIG!' Bagby dropped his totem, smearing the glistening slop from his cheek. 'I didn't want to summon a dirty old wilderpig!'

Pena laughed. 'You look good together!' she exclaimed, pinching her nose from the smell. 'It needs a name! How about Stinkbag?'

'OINK!' Stinkbag seemed to agree.

'OINK OINK!' Boja yelled from his bed of flattened flowers. He waved his arms excitedly in the air. 'OINK! OINK! OINK!'

'No! No, oink!' Bagby wailed with frustration. He stamped his feet. 'Shoo, Stinkbag! SHOO!'

Stinkbag the wilderpig flumped on to its

hairy bottom and stared mournfully back at Bagby, only for Bagby to cross his arms and harrumph. So, slowly, reluctantly, Stinkbag the wilderpig wobbled back on to his trotters and started to walk away, stopping only once to glance back, before disappearing between the flowers completely.

Elder Nakobe took Bagby's totem from his hands, and bonked him on the head with it. 'All animals attracted to flember,' she grumbled, handing his totem back. 'Flember is *life*. But flember animal . . . comes from Flember Stream itself.'

She stood in front of Pena and nodded expectantly.

Pena took a deep breath. Then she closed her eyes. She held her totem out amongst the flowers. And she started to whisper.

'I would like a deer,' she wished. 'A beautiful, glowing flember deer.'

Her totem started to glow ever so faintly. Then she knelt down, lowering it closer to the ground. 'A deer. Bring me a *deer*.'

Dev watched around her, for any sign of the roots beneath the soil, for any glowing creatures slinking through the flowers. But, as long as he waited, nothing appeared. And after a while, Elder Nakobe rested a hand gently on Pena's shoulder.

She opened her eyes, smiling politely at Elder Nakobe. 'I tried,' she sighed, her voice quivering with disappointment.

Elder Nakobe clasped Pena's totem between her hands. '*Se se chonokay*,' she muttered. 'It will find you . . . when you are *ready*.'

Then she turned to Dev.

'Your turn.'

'I . . . I still don't have a . . .' Dev started, only for Elder Nakobe to thrust her own totem towards him. It felt thick, sturdy, the glow fading from its lantern as soon as he clasped his hands around it.

'Borrow.' Elder Nakobe smiled. 'See how you do.'

'Come on then, Dev.' Santoro sat down in the long grass, a grin plastered across his face. 'She's trusted you with her own stick, so maybe you'd better summon something.'

Dev felt nervous. He cleared his throat, as if he was about to make a speech, then he held Elder Nakobe's totem out in front of him. 'So I just . . . I close my eyes?' he asked. 'And then how do I . . . *connect* . . . with the Flember Stream?'

Elder Nakobe leant in close. She lifted her hand and closed Dev's eyes with her own fingers. 'Use totem . . . like a *bridge*,' she whispered. 'Bridge between you and ground.'

Gradually, Dev allowed his breathing to become slow. Calm. His mind started to clear. He wasn't quite sure whether he should be saying anything, or imagining anything, so he concentrated on the totem he was holding, the way it felt between his hands. How it might look if it was glowing.

Then he felt Elder Nakobe lean in even closer.

'Now,' she whispered. 'Reach *across* bridge.'

Suddenly, Dev could feel it.

He could feel flember flowing beneath his feet. The quiet hum of the grass. The swaying of the flowers. The slow stretching of plant roots below the gentle heave of the soil.

'Um, Dev . . .' His brother gasped.

Dev peeked between his closed eyelids to see the totem's lantern was glowing. Only a little, but it was *something*. He then turned it, so the lantern was touching the ground. Light ebbed out around his boots, then sank down, beneath the soil, a thin, twisted bundle of roots glowing below his feet.

'I'm doing it.' He beamed. 'I'm summoning flember!'

'Oh, well, that totem works WAY better!' Bagby cried rather ungraciously, only for his sister to shush him down.

Dev looked over to Elder Nakobe. She stared back at him, her eyes wide, shimmering in the light from the totem. 'You are . . . quick to learn,' she whispered, as if hardly able to believe what she was seeing.

Dev let out an exhilarated laugh. 'What do I do now?' he cried. 'What next?'

Elder Nakobe pointed down to the glowing roots. 'Flember guides the way,' she said. 'So *follow* it.'

8

The Deepest Roots

Dev held Elder Nakobe's totem out in front of him and ploughed his way through the meadow. The roots in the ground were thin, and no glowing mushrooms were poking out from them, but he could still follow their wispy trail between the flowers, then away from the flowers, down a long, sloping hill, and into the shadow of the tall trees.

Where the air blew cooler.

The leaves rustled noisily around him.

And the roots faded away at the edge of a deep, cavernous drop.

He peered down into the darkness. The trail had, for some reason, brought him to a crater in the ground,

which disappeared into a tumble of rocks and dead tree trunks. It looked so dark down there, so dangerous, as if it hadn't felt the warmth of flember for many, many years.

Elder Nakobe walked alongside him. She took the totem from his hands, and planted it down on the rocky ground.

'Some roots . . .' An excitement twinkled in her eye. '*Joh joh senteh* . . . They run *deeper* than others.'

Faint cracks of light started to glimmer in the darkness. Cracks which then spread, then split apart. They rose, reaching between the rocks, light shimmering across everything they touched. Thick dewy grass sprouted around them, from which sprang bushes, then trees.

Glistening brooks trickled between it all, before spilling down into a wide pool of crystal clear water.

Insects started to click. Birds started to tweet.

Life yawned out below Dev's feet.

And all he could do was stare at it, utterly stunned.

'She's doing it again!' Bagby barged past Dev, shoving the heavy cloak from around his shoulders. It FLOMP-ed to the ground. Then, with a laugh, he flung himself into the air, curling up into a ball before plummeting down into the waters below with a loud SPLASH!

Pena unhooked her bow, her arrows, threw off her hat, and raced after her brother. 'Elder Nakobe looks for places that don't have much flember!' she cried, somersaulting off the edge of the crater. 'Then she brings them back to LIFE!'

SPLOOSH! She plunged into the waters.

'Gotta say, after all the walking we've done, jumping into a pond sounds like a pretty sweet idea,' Santoro said, slipping off his sword and his armour as he followed Bagby and Pena down towards the water. His descent, however, was more careful, climbing down the inside of the crater, carefully jumping from one tree root to another. That is, until the huge, round, giggling shape of Boja suddenly rolled down towards him like a boulder. Santoro barely had a chance to yelp before the bear's huge red butt FLOOMPH-ed him in the face, and sent them both tumbling down into the water with an almighty SPLO-O-O-O-O-SH!

The mighty waves sent Bagby and Pena rolling against the pond's edge. They laughed, hysterically, as Boja poked his head above the surface with a giant lily pad flopped across his eyes. Santoro followed, spitting out great mouthfuls of water, choking a few curse words in the bear's general direction.

Dev sat down, dangling his legs over the crater's edge. He watched Santoro and Boja with a cheer in his heart. Then he took a deep breath of the cool, fresh air. 'So you can summon flember even where there doesn't seem to be any?'

With a few puffs and grunts, Elder Nakobe sat down beside him. 'Yes,' she replied. 'But only if you can find Flember Stream.' She pointed her totem down towards the water. There, beneath a row of hanging whistletrees, Dev spotted something made of stone poking out from beneath the surface. He stood, and walked around the crater for a better view.

'What is *that*?' Dev asked.

'*Finjay sheh*,' Elder Nakobe called back. 'It is a . . . *temple*. Long time ago . . . elders build temples along Flember Stream. To protect. Flember is . . . *shinokay* . . .

69

light. We . . . *protect* light.'

She stared at Dev intensely, and she nodded. 'Where there is no light,' she warned. 'Darkness grows.'

Elder Nakobe tilted her head towards the skies again. Dev did too. He listened for the breeze, but he could hear nothing. No birds. Not in the sky, nor nestled in the trees of the crater. The insects had stopped buzzing. Even the splashing from the pond below faded away, as an eerie silence fell upon them all.

Nakobe turned back to Dev. Her eyes were wide. Her face drained of all its colour.

She looked very, very worried.

'We have to go,' she whispered. '*Skraw* is here!'

9

The Skraw

'DEV?' Santoro shouted. 'Dev, Boja's going weird!'

Dev glanced down to the pond. There stood Boja, water up to his waist, lily pad flopping from his head like a posh lady's hat. He was comple-e-e-etely still. His eyes wide. His ears pricked back. His flember bristling across his fur.

And then Dev heard it. A sound he'd heard before. A noise like no other. It rattled through his bones, sent goosebumps across his skin. It turned his arms and legs to jelly. 'That music,' Dev muttered, as it grew louder, and louder. 'I've heard it before!'

Suddenly, the creature he'd seen on the cliff edge slammed down in front of him, barging messily against Elder Nakobe. She staggered back, her feet losing their hold as she slipped from the crater's edge. CRASH! SMASH! THUNK! Her shelves smashed against the rocks, pots and pans sent flying into the air before THUMP! She landed on a small patch of grass, rolling beneath the leaves of a hanging willow tree.

Where she lay, motionless.

The creature's leafy robes swirled around its body as it CRACK-CRACK-CRACK-ed its crooked body to full height. It loomed over Dev. Its beak glinting in the sunlight. Its eyes glowing a furious red.

'N . . . Nakobe called you a *Skraw*,' Dev stammered, his whole body shaking. 'Are you . . . are you here for *me*?'

THUNK! THUNK THUNK! The creature's long, metal tendrils spun out from beneath its cloak. They embedded themselves into the grass, sucking the flember up to leave only crinkled, dead ashes in its wake. Bright crackles of light swarmed across the creature's body. But they would not hold. Dev could feel flember escaping, crackling back towards the ground, reviving the grass once more as if the creature couldn't hold on to it.

'You're struggling, Skraw.' A confidence spiked in Dev's chest. He took his chance. He grabbed a large clump of soil and flung it into the creature's face, knocking it backwards. With a speed that surprised even himself, Dev then skidded between its tendrils, throwing himself down inside the crater. Gripping one thick root after another, slipping, tripping, then collapsing on to the grass beside Elder Nakobe. He unhooked the smashed remains of her shelves, grabbed her in his arms, and pulled her further into the shade. Her skin was bruised. Her eyes closed. He listened. She was still breathing, but it was very shallow.

'HWOOOARGHH!' Boja suddenly boomed over the music that was still filling the air. Dev turned to see the huge red bear raising his paws above his head. His eyes, his huge, bulging eyes, usually glowing with the crackling blue light of flember, now glowed a furious swirling red that sparkled like lightning behind his pupils. His body, too, already alight with an excess of flember, cast a terrifying red glow around the inside of the crater.

He staggered, disorientated, back and forth. Mumbling under his breath. Almost *humming* along with the music.

Then he turned towards Bagby and Pena.

Both of them shrieked with fear. The rocks were too slippery for them to grab on to and climb out of the water, so all they could do was huddle against them, desperately clinging on to each other as Boja marched closer. And closer. His face scrunched up into a snarl. His bright red flember trailed across the water's surface.

Then, suddenly, a long knotted vine FLOMP-ed over his head, pulling taut beneath his nose, and yanking his whole head back. Santoro stood behind him, armour glowing, as he clutched each end of the vine.

'You don't seem your usual self,' he growled, struggling to rein the bear back.

Boja turned, fists balled, and started wading back towards Santoro. Santoro's determination wavered. He dropped his vine lasso in the water. Panic washed across his face. 'Devvvv?' Santoro yelled, backing slowly away. 'What's WRONG with BOJA?'

'It must be the . . . *music*!' Dev shouted over the noise. 'Somehow the music is affecting him!' He pointed towards Boja's big, bushy red eyebrows. Although they were bunched into a furious frown, they were twitching – up and down, up and down – in time with all the clanging, the honks, the beeps and the calamitous tinkling.

'The music seems to have turned Boja *against us*!'

Elder Nakobe let out a splutter, snapping Dev's attention back towards her. Then he saw something beneath the bushes. There was something . . . wiggling . . . underneath. It looked like toes. Wiggly little toes, on a wiggly little foot. Dev slowly lifted his head to see Pockle nestled in amongst the leaves.

'POCKLE!' She beamed, creeping out from the bush. 'You found me!'

'Pockle, no! Not now! It's not safe!' Dev cried. 'Hide again! HIDE!'

'GOLLUP!' Gollup burped, poking out from on top of her head. Pockle reached up and grabbed him, carefully placing him down on the ground, before lifting the leafy, muddy flaps of her headdress so she could hear what Dev was saying. Only now, it seemed, could she also hear the pounding music. She winced at the noise. Then she saw Elder Nakobe huddled behind Dev, and the smile started to wither from her face completely.

'Elder Nakobe are you . . . are you asleep?' she asked nervously.

Dev was about to reach out, to hold on to Pockle, to keep her safe, when he caught sight of something which made his heart sink into the pit of his belly.

Tendrils, writhing out from between the trees.

As the dark shadow of the Skraw rose up behind Pockle.

'NO!' Elder Nakobe suddenly shouted, lunging between Dev and Pockle, thrusting her totem out above them. Its lantern glowed with the beautiful blue light of flember, shining brighter, and brighter, as she pointed it towards the Skraw. '*Rojinjay te te so flominjay!*' she cried above the music. '*ROJINJAY TE TE SO FLOMINJAY!*'

By its light, Dev saw movement in the trees around them. Their branches swayed, their thick roots started to bulge, the rocks they held in place started to dislodge. The ground beneath Dev's boots started to rumble.

The Skraw, however, did not seem afraid. It leant forwards, reaching over Pockle as it clamped its claws around Nakobe's totem. Swirls of flember started to wisp out from it, then from Nakobe herself. Her eyes opened wide. The colour drained from her cheeks. Her whole body started to crumple.

Suddenly, the Skraw let go of Nakobe's totem. Its thick

claws wrapped around Pockle instead. Pockle looked up, confused, unsure of quite what she was looking at. 'Who summoned *you*?' she asked, gingerly reaching out towards its beak.

The Skraw's arms slid a little tighter around her. Then two long, torn wings stretched out from behind it, flapped to their full length, and in an instant it was carrying her out of the crater, and up into the sky.

A trail of flember crackling out behind it.

The music faded.

Dev fell alongside Nakobe.

'POCKLE!' he cried, clutching Elder Nakobe's frail, shivering body. 'THAT . . . *THING*! THAT *SKRAW*! IT TOOK POCKLE!'

10

Safety

As the music disappeared into the clouds, Boja's mood started to settle. The bear slumped in the water just inches away from Santoro, puffing, wheezing, his fur ruffling itself flat again. All the red drained from his flember.

All his anger was gone.

He looked exhausted.

Bagby and Pena carefully edged around the pond, climbing back on to land before rushing towards Elder Nakobe. They both hugged her tightly. Gollup emerged from the hedges, nervously golluping as it slithered between them, before nestling on Nakobe's lap. She rested her hands on him, drawing a glowing light from his body. Dev took a few steps back. Now Elder Nakobe had people around her, he could clamber down towards the pond, check Santoro was OK, then check on the tired bear.

'Dev, he went CRAZY!' Santoro cried as Dev got closer to Boja. 'He wanted to grab us! I don't know why!'

Boja opened his mouth to respond. At first only a burble-burble-burble came out, which slowly settled into a word.

'Soh-rry,' he sighed sheepishly.

'Well his flember's settled back down,' Dev muttered, carefully widening Boja's eyelids and watching his pupils shrink. 'I can run some tests, make sure he's OK.' Dev looked inside the bear's ears. Poked a finger up his nose.

Listened to the DOOMPF-DOOMPF-DOOMPF of Boja's golden heart pounding weakly inside his chest. Then he opened up Boja's mouth, and pulled out his tongue. It looked its normal pink rubbery self, except for a few odd black marks along the side of it.

'CAMP!' Bagby suddenly shouted. He leant in closer to Elder Nakobe's moving lips. 'Elder Nakobe says to take her back to the camp!'

Tears welled in Pena's eyes. 'But what about Pockle? We have to look for POCKLE!'

'Nakobe says CAMP,' Bagby snapped. 'We do what she says. We can work it out from there!'

'Well, what do we do with Boja?' Santoro huffed, eyeing the guilty-looking bear suspiciously. 'We can't trust him not to turn on us again.'

'He's not coming with *us*!' Pena shouted tearfully.

Dev reached down beneath the water and pulled up a fistful of wet, silty mud. 'Don't worry about Boja,' he insisted. 'I have a plan.'

By the time Dev had led them all back to the camp – using a combination of the map inside the flember book, vague memory, a few unsuccessful attempts with Nakobe's totem, and quite a bit of blind luck – late afternoon was falling upon the Wildening. Strange glowing insects clicked in the low light. Even stranger howls sounded from the distance. And a cold wind carried it all, fighting against the flaming torches along the fence.

Boja, his ears stuffed full of wet mud so he wouldn't be able to hear the music if the Skraw appeared again, had been tasked with carrying Elder Nakobe's frail body. He was only too happy to help. The only downside was that now Boja couldn't hear *anything*, sending Dev running after him whenever he wandered in the wrong direction.

'In here,' Dev beckoned Boja through the camp's open gate.

'Wha?' Boja smiled politely. 'Can't . . . hear.'

Dev held out Nakobe's totem, and gestured to one of the huts. 'Place Elder Nakobe down there, against the wall,' he said, guiding Boja. 'Carefully. Be very gentle.'

'Now step away!' Bagby snapped. Santoro shooed Boja back. With the bear at a safe distance, they all huddled around Elder Nakobe.

Her eyes were closed. Her breathing shallow.

She clutched tightly on to a sleeping Gollup.

'We need to find Pockle,' Pena insisted, glaring at Boja as she wiped her tear-soaked cheeks. 'We need to find Pockle, so we need to find the SKRAW!'

'The Skraw is a myth,' Bagby cursed, folding his arms across his chest. 'A story grown-ups tell children to make sure they don't go wandering off into the Wildening. It's not real. That . . . that thing we saw. It was something else. A wild animal or something!'

Pena broke down into sobs. The sight of her brought tears back into Bagby's eyes.

'It . . . it *can't* be real,' he blubbed.

Dev wrapped an arm around Bagby's shoulders, pulling him a little closer towards Pena. He tried to think of something reassuring, to comfort them both, but he didn't quite have the words.

All he could do was try to stop his own lip from wobbling.

Elder Nakobe mumbled something. They all crouched down beside her, Pena gripping her hand. 'Elder Nakobe, what do we DO?' she whispered. 'We're not trained to deal with any of this! And we're too far away from home to get help!'

Elder Nakobe's eyes opened slightly. She scanned them all, resting her gaze upon Dev. 'Totem,' she whispered. Dev carefully placed the totem into her hands. She held it as straight as she could manage, and, as she did, its lantern started to glow. A soft blue light ebbed out from it, sinking down, across the ground, circling them all, poking tiny colourful flowers up from the bare soil.

A nervous smile crept into Dev's cheeks. He noticed

Elder Nakobe was smiling too, nodding, as if answering a question no one else could hear.

'Are you . . . are you connecting to the Flember Stream?' Dev asked hopefully. 'Can you use it to heal yourself?'

Elder Nakobe looked at him in the flickering light of her totem. '*Soh soh nejay*,' she muttered, holding the totem out towards Dev.

'I'm sorry, I don't . . .'

'She wants you to take it,' Pena said.

'Oh, no,' Dev insisted. 'Elder Nakobe, you need it right now, it's yours!'

Elder Nakobe's smile widened between the creases of her face.

'Don't need it,' she replied. 'Not any more.' Again she thrust it towards Dev. He tentatively wrapped his hands around its staff, and as he did, Elder Nakobe's hold weakened. The light from the totem started to fade.

'No no no.' Pena winced, pressing her face closer to Nakobe's. 'Stay with us, *please* stay with us.'

'*Pajoba*,' Elder Nakobe whispered. 'Go home. *Seh seh*. Home.'

'We don't know the way!' Bagby cried.

Elder Nakobe looked over to Dev. Dev stared back, mouth agape, still clutching her totem. Still looking rather confused.

'*He* will guide you,' she said.

'Dev? Dev doesn't know the way either!' Santoro coughed, holding back his own tears.

Elder Nakobe cast her gaze around them all one more

time, then slowly closed her eyes. The grass beneath her started to plumpen. The flowers billowed out further. Life spilled around them all like the water splashing from a puddle.

'*Seh seh*,' she whispered in the faintest of voices. 'He knows *enough* now.'

As her body relaxed, Gollup slowly, sleepily, slid down from her belly, and on to the ground. Bagby and Pena both let out a panicked cry, grabbing on to Nakobe's robes and shaking her, trying desperately to wake her up again.

'DO something!' Santoro nudged Boja urgently. Still, Boja couldn't hear what he was saying, but he got the gist. Against Bagby and Pena's protests, the big red bear stumbled forwards, rubbing his paws together as the sparkling light of his flember crackled across his fur. He gently gripped Nakobe's hands, his flember swaying back and forth across her arms. But nothing, nothing was waking her. Nothing would stir the colour back into her cheeks.

Dev could only stare at the grass bustling around them.

'I'm sorry,' his voice trembled. 'I think she's gone.'

11

A Goodbye

Pena collapsed into tears. Bagby tried to hold his in a little longer, but soon their sobbing was echoing up into the night sky. Dev, too, could feel the tears welling up in his eyes, but his brother was quick to wrap him into a hug, just as a large set of red arms squeezed around them both.

At which point Dev pressed his face into Boja's belly fur, and he burst into tears.

'Soh-rry,' Boja repeated, for maybe the twentieth time, as a large, glistening teardrop worked its way loose from his eye and splashed down against Dev's helmet. Santoro, however, pulled himself away from them both. He

87

smeared his own tears away with his wrists, and stared at Boja with a deep suspicion.

'Music or not, I'm not letting you out of my sight, Boja,' Santoro warned, defiantly flicking the hair from his eyes. 'I'll leave you behind if you turn on us again, I'd do anything to keep Dev safe!'

Boja lifted a paw, and pointed towards his mud-filled ears.

'Can't . . .'

'Can't hear, yeah yeah,' Santoro huffed. 'I'm still watching you.'

Like his brother, Dev had also been worrying about their situation. After all, what were they supposed to do now? Pockle was missing. Bagby and Pena were alone. Dev and Santoro themselves were being followed not only by the dark wolves, but by some horrible creature trying to suck flember from the ground. And Boja, the one bear they thought they could rely on, now seemed to be *glitching*.

Dev stared at the totem in his hand, wishing it would glow like it did before. Because right now the world felt very lonely.

And the evening was growing very, very dark.

Santoro loudly cleared his throat. 'In Eden, we . . . we have a tradition,' he said, 'when someone we love returns their flember to the earth.'

Bagby and Pena looked up, sniffling. Pena had bundled Gollup into a tight hug, the three of them still pressed as close as possible to Elder Nakobe's body.

'It is a way for us to give thanks,' Santoro continued, gesturing for Dev to stand alongside him. 'To show our appreciation for how they carried their flember throughout their life.'

'Jikanda.' Dev nodded.

'Exactly.'

With some delicacy, Dev gently eased Bagby, Pena and Gollup away from Elder Nakobe. On Dev's repeated and mimed instructions, Boja slid his paws under her body, lifted her up into his arms, then carried her over to a patch of long grass at the darker end of the camp. He placed Nakobe down on to the ground. Then, with long swipes of his huge paws, he started to dig out a large hole beside her. Dev lit more torches around him, while Santoro held Bagby and Pena's hands, and when it was decided Boja had dug a hole deep enough, Elder Nakobe's body was gently lowered inside.

While still hugging Gollup under one arm, Pena

carried a bunch of dried flowers under the other, and laid them tearfully upon Nakobe's chest. Bagby followed, pulling the bracelet of tiny bones from his wrist, then placing it beside the flowers.

Both of them being careful not to step too close to Boja.

Dev thought maybe it was his turn to offer something. He went to plant Nakobe's totem in the earth by her feet, until Pena stopped him.

'She said it was for you, it is a great honour for an elder to give their totem.' She cast Dev a fragile smile.

'Whatever her reasons, she wanted you to have it.'

Dev nodded, and took a few steps back. Then he gestured to Boja, who slowly, carefully, shovelled the earth back over Elder Nakobe, until the hole was completely filled in.

'We say these words,' Dev said quietly. '*Jikanda jokay . . .*'

'. . . *jijin te sep,*' Bagby and Pena mumbled.

'You . . . you know the tradition?'

'It's a *Wildening* tradition,' Bagby grumbled, wiping his arm across his nose with a loud SNI-I-I-I-IFFLE. '*Jikanda jokay, jijin te sep.*'

The breeze picked up around them. Vines swayed. Tree branches bowed down towards where they had laid Elder Nakobe.

Everything was peaceful.

Everything was calm.

It felt, at least to Dev, as if the island itself was paying its respects.

Santoro leant in a little closer to his brother. 'Dev, I don't know what we should do now,' he whispered under his breath. For the first time, Santoro looked nervous. He looked lost. Santoro Everdew, Dev's cool, confident, older brother, was looking to *him* for guidance.

'We have to help them.' Dev lowered his voice,

watching Bagby and Pena closely. 'I thought that thing . . . that Skraw . . . was coming for me, but it wasn't. I think it just wanted flember. It tried to suck it out of the ground, but then it took Pockle instead. I don't know why, and I don't know where it went, but with Elder Nakobe gone we're Bagby and Pena's best chance of ever finding her again.'

Santoro sighed, running a hand through his hair. 'I really thought we were going home,' he replied.

'Pajoba,' Bagby interrupted with a whisper. 'That's where we live. It's the citadel north from here but, uh, Elder Nakobe hasn't really taught us how to navigate yet.'

Something glimmered inside Dev's mind. *Pajoba!* He recognized that name. Quickly, he pulled the flember book from his backpack, flicked to the later chapters, and lit up the map.

'THERE!' he cried, pointing out the glowing letters across the page. 'Dad knew Pajoba. He marked it on the map!'

'If we can get back there, then we can tell everyone what happened, and we can tell the elder council.' An enthusiasm stirred in Pena's voice. Gollup yawned a sweet belch from under her arm, much to Boja's delight.

'Then we can all go and find Pockle *together*.' Dev beamed.

Santoro nodded. 'Well, if we are all going back into the Wildening, the wolves might still be out there, the *Skraw* might still be out there. You're really going to need to learn how to defend yourself, Dev. No inventions. No weird ideas. Just good, honest, Guild-level training.'

'Too late.' A wry smile crept across Dev's cheek. 'I've already had the *weirdest* idea.'

12

A Vehicle

Dev's mind started to whirr.

His idea was taking shape.

He glanced around the camp – from the flickering torches, to the abandoned cart, the broken furniture, across the swaying reeds to the thick hanging ropes. And then his gaze landed upon the smaller hut Boja had knocked over when he first arrived. Its wall still held the distinctive imprint of his buttocks.

And suddenly, like a flame sparking in a field of dry grass, every thought Dev was having blazed together as one.

He gripped the cart handles and, with some effort, hauled the cart out from the long grass. 'Santoro, I can

get us to Pajoba safely, but I'm going to need help. Can you get these wheels off, and fix them up? I need all four of them. Use reeds, leather, straw, switch the spokes out with sticks, it doesn't matter how you do it, we just need *wheels.*'

Santoro let out a low, breathy growl.

'Dev, you need to protect yourself . . .'

'I'm going to protect *all* of us,' Dev insisted. 'Santoro, PLEASE.'

Dev then turned to Boja. Boja smiled cautiously back. 'Boja, we need this,' Dev announced, pointing at the small hut lying on its side. 'I need you to pick it up. The whole thing.'

Boja stared blankly at the hut.

'Pick it up!' Dev mimed the action of picking up a hut as best he could.

'OH!' Boja saluted, accidentally slapping himself in the eye, before wrapping his big red arms around the hut, and he-e-e-eaving it off the ground.

Dev turned to Bagby and Pena. 'I know this is tough,' he said, as their eyes glistened in the flickering torch-light. 'But I need both of you to help me. Pena, we're going to need supplies, any food you have in the camp. And, Bagby, I need the *fizzleplop paste.*' He pointed to the bowls of brightly coloured pink paste lining the path. 'Gather it all up carefully, and we'll take it with us. It might be our best weapon if we're attacked again.'

Bagby and Pena both nodded. Gollup, hanging from Pena's arms, let out a long sleepy yawn, only for a loud CRA-A-A-ASH to startle him awake. Boja was gripping the small hut up against his chest. Bowls, crates and cutlery clattered out from inside it. Through a tall swirl of dust, Boja turned to show Dev.

'DID IT!' Boja beamed.

'Now FLIP it!'

'UH?'

'FLIP IT!' Dev mimed.

In one slick move, Boja flipped the hut upside down, and dropped it on to its roof. Thankfully the hut was sturdy, crumpling around the edges but still holding its shape.

'THANK YOU BOJA!' Dev cried with delight.

'S'OK!' Boja yelled back.

Dev paused.

Boja had heard him. Clearly the mud in his ears was losing its effect.

Dev ran to the boundary of the camp, reached up, and grabbed two large fistfuls of leaves from the tree branches. Then he returned, climbed up Boja's back, and thrust them all inside the bear's muddy red ears.

'CAN YOU HEAR ME NOW?' Dev yelled over the rustle of the leaves.

Boja stared into space.

Then PR-R-R-P-P-ed out a fart.

'I think we're safe,' Dev puffed, clambering back down.

'Wheels are ready.' Santoro clutched four large wheels. He had done as well as he could, replacing the broken spokes and patching them all up with clay.

He stared in bemusement at the upside down hut.

'I don't know what this plan is,' he sighed. 'But it's going to be ridiculous isn't it?'

'Of course it is.' Dev nodded. 'The best ideas always are!'

INVENTION 512: The Hut-On-Wheels

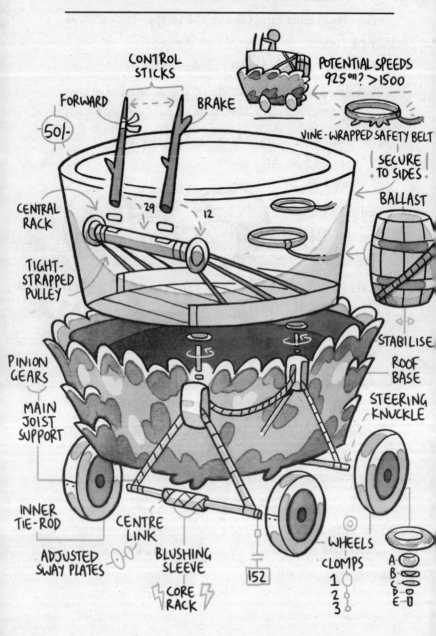

CONTROL STICKS

FORWARD

BRAKE

POTENTIAL SPEEDS
925 oʰ? >1500

50/-

VINE-WRAPPED SAFETY BELT

SECURE
TO SIDES

BALLAST

CENTRAL RACK

29   12

TIGHT-STRAPPED PULLEY

STABILISE

ROOF BASE

PINION GEARS

STEERING KNUCKLE

MAIN JOIST SUPPORT

INNER TIE-ROD

CENTRE LINK

ADJUSTED SWAY PLATES

BLUSHING SLEEVE

CORE RACK

152

WHEELS

CLOMPS
1
2
3

A
B
C
D
E

CHOMPTATO

13

Leaving the Camp

'IS EVERYONE STRAPPED IN?' Dev called out. The Hut-On-Wheels stood at the very edge of the camp, with Dev perched at its helm. It hadn't been an easy construction – sticking wheels to an upside down hut required frames to be built around it, pulleys, a whole network of vines pulled taut into a steering rack – and Dev knew that despite everything he had done, it would still be a bumpy ride. Which is why, as one final touch, he had installed safety belts.

Bagby and Pena both pulled on theirs. 'I'm in,' Bagby grumbled, packages of pink paste strapped in tightly behind him. 'But I don't want to be sat next to that . . . that *monster*.'

Boja, with five different safety belts pulled across his belly and leaves stuffed inside his ears, couldn't hear what Bagby had just called him. So instead he raised his fists in the air, and cheered an excited 'WHOOOO!'

'If he really *must* come with us . . .' Pena was nestled between Bagby and a sack filled with chomptatoes: weird, knobbly, root vegetables. She tucked the ever-sleepy Gollup a little further down inside her cloak. 'Then can we hurry up? Pockle's out there somewhere, and we can't waste any more time!'

Santoro pulled his own belt across his armoured chestplate. 'Dev,' he mumbled, wearily. 'Are we sure this is the best idea? If we take these two back out into the Wildening we might come up against the dark wolves again, or that *Skraw*!'

'I hope we do!' Bagby proclaimed. 'If that thing comes back for us I'm gonna hit it with my hitting stick. Now let's go get POCKLE!'

He pulled one of the vegetables from the sack, and took a huge bite out of it.

'Before I eatsch all of feh chomptatoesch,' he coughed.

Dev nodded to Santoro, trying to look brave, while ignoring the sound of his own heartbeat hammering in his ears. 'Elder Nakobe told us to go to Pajoba,' he said, reaching into his backpack and pulling out the flember book. He handed it over to Santoro. 'So I'll drive, you read the map. The sooner we get there, the sooner we'll all be safe again.'

He tucked Nakobe's totem beside him, then pushed down hard on the two levers between his boots. With a loud CRE-E-E-EAK, the Hut-On-Wheels slowly rolled forward. Everyone inside clung on to something. Santoro clung on to the book. Bagby clung on to Santoro. Pena clung on to Gollup. Boja clung on to Bagby's chomptato. Then he carefully freed it from Bagby's hands, and slowly guided it towards his mouth. Dev cast one last glance to the camp, catching sight of the orange glowing torches as they fizzled out behind the trees. 'We'll look after them, Nakobe,' he whispered under his breath. 'I promise we'll get them h . . . O-O-O-O-O-ARGHHHH!'

Suddenly, the slope of the ground steepened, sending the Hut-On-Wheels rattling forwards under its own momentum. 'HWOOO-O-O-O-O-O-O-OARGHH!' Boja agreed, as they sped faster, and *faster* – between the trees, over the bumpy ground. Everyone inside the hut HWOOO-O-O-O-O-O-OARGH-ing together, until a cluster of thick, low-hanging leaves whipped against their faces, the trees ran out, and they were left whizzing across a wide, rocky clearing. Their terrified faces lit by the huge, white moon shining above.

'D-D-D-D-Dev, I c-c-c-c-can't s-s-s-see where we're g-g-g-going,' Santoro stammered, frantically trying to hold the flember book pages flat.

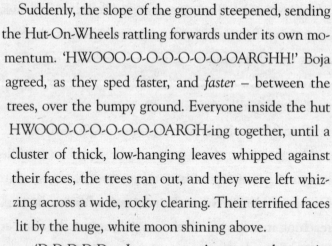

Dev unclenched his white knuckles from the levers. Carefully, very, very

carefully, he took the pages, then pressed the glowing F upon them. 'B-B-B-Bagby said we should head n-n-north,' he shouted back, following the map. 'N-n-orth leads us straight t-t-to . . .'

Boja suddenly shrieked again.

This, however, was not an excited HWOARGH.

Dev looked up to see the ground disappear some distance in front of them, with only a dark sky lying beyond. 'DEAD DROP CANYON!' Dev screamed, as he fumbled the book closed and pulled hard on the levers.

The whole hut lurched to one side. Its makeshift brake pads SCRE-E-E-E-EECH-ed loudly, painfully, forcing everyone to cover their ears.

'Lean!' Dev yelled. 'EVERYBODY LEAN!'

Everyone leant to one side, and their combined weight tilted the hut up on to two wheels. With only inches to spare it skimmed the top of the canyon, skidding perilously close to the crumbling edge and carving a wide arc in the ground behind it. Dev's teeth chattered, his bones rattled. He reached out, desperately heaving the lever as far as it would go until – CHKKK! – it snapped off in his hand.

He held it up in disbelief.

'That . . . that was the brake stick!' he cried, as Santoro yelled something rude into the wind. Fortunately for them all, however, the canyon's edge was starting to dip. The ground sloped downwards, carrying the hut into the low-ceilinged caverns carved into the rockface itself. The hut's other two wheels bounced back on to the ground. Dev let out a loud 'WHEWWW!' of relief.

But their problems were far from over.

With all wheels on the ground, and no brake, the hut started to pick up speed again. It raced through the caverns, as Boja's head CLONK-CLONK-CLONK-ed against the rocky stalactites, before they suddenly shot out into a wide stretch of forest unlike anything Dev had ever seen before.

An unnatural light hit the huge, thick trees. It made them look grey, no, silvery, their oily bark shimmering beneath the moon. Very few, however, were still standing. Most lay fallen, forming a dangerously random path, twisting and winding down between two narrowing walls of rock.

Santoro gripped tightly on to Dev's shoulders.

'D-D-Dev, is this the right way?'

'R-r-r-right now it's the only way!' Dev yelled back.

'WHOOOOO!' Boja yelled over both of them. Once again he was utterly delighted by everything that was happening. He squeaked, and cheered, and roared with excitement, as they clattered across the curved bridge of a fallen tree. Dev, however, wasn't so thrilled. He peered down into the deep, dark drop below them. A hollow sense of dread filled his body. Then, a sudden jolt of panic, as the hut skidded on the slippery bark. Dev hung on tightly as they leant one way, then the other, before spinning around completely.

Boja was now at the front. Albeit facing the wrong way.

'Boja, slow us down!' Dev yelled. 'Hold your arms out!' He gestured to the towering walls of rock whizzing past. 'Try to grab on to something!'

Boja grinned, oblivious, still excited by the ride.

'GRAB ON TO SOMETHING!' Dev shouted.

Boja, suddenly realizing what he was meant to do, stretched his arms out either side of him. His big red fingertips scraped along the rocks, hooking on to roots, branches, snapping them as he grabbed.

'It's working!' Santoro cheered. 'Dev, he's slowing us down!'

Then, suddenly, it didn't matter. The trunk ran out. Boja's fingers lost their hold. The hut was flipped up a ramp of tangled roots, smashing hard against the rock opposite, then rolling down a slope of fallen boulders. It landed into wet, slippery gravel with a loud CRUNCH.

Crumpled.

But in one piece.

With everyone still strapped safely inside.

14
Prey

'Well, the wheels are ruined,' Santoro said, picking at the smashed remains of his own hard work. Dev, however, was quiet. He stood in the dripping cavern, staring at the Hut-On-Wheels, his face scrunched into a thoughtful frown.

'May-y-y-be we don't need wheels . . .' he mused, gazing towards the big red bear still sitting inside it.

'Where even ARE we?' Pena lowered herself down from the hut. She peeked inside her cloak, carefully tending to Gollup who, it appeared, had slept through their entire ordeal.

She lowered her voice to a hush. 'We must have gone way off course!'

'I don't recognize anything here.' Bagby knelt down and sniffed the ground. He appeared to be looking for a scent. His nose led him crawling, snuffling across the gravel, up towards a large crack in the rocky walls. Beyond it rolled trees, grass, hills, all lit up by the bright moonlight. Bagby sniffed the cool night air as it breezed in. 'Nope,' he proclaimed, fiddling with the buttons of his cloak. 'This is all new to me. I'd better just mark it now.'

'What's he doing?' Santoro whispered.

Pena sighed and rolled her eyes. 'Bagby pees everywhere he goes. Like he's leaving his scent. He says it helps him find his way around.'

As Pena and Santoro both turned their heads in disgust, a growl interrupted them all. A low, snarling growl which grew around the cavern, sending shivers down Dev's spine, and a weakness through his bones.

'A dark wolf,' Santoro snarled back. 'There's one in here!'

Santoro reached back for his sword handle, pulling the blade out into the light of his own glowing armour. He stood there, ear cocked, listening to the growls. All of a sudden, he swung his sword towards the darkest corner of the cavern.

Just as a jagged, black shape slowly slunk out from the shadows.

Pena pulled out her bow, then an arrow from her quiver. The arrow fizzed a gentle pink as it rubbed against the bow, but Pena's hands were trembling too much to hold it steady.

'DEV!' Santoro yelled over his shoulder. 'We're going to hold it off, but you need to . . .'

The words blurred in Dev's ears. The scratches on his arm were throbbing again. His head was swimming. His legs felt like jelly. This close to the dark wolf, he was struggling to keep it together.

'I . . . I'm on it,' he stammered, unconvincingly. With some effort he hauled himself back into the hut, then reached down inside its inner workings. He yanked out all of its unnecessary gears, then dropped down to the straw roof, which he started pounding with his foot.

'Boja!' Dev gestured. 'I need your help!'

Boja beamed, unlocking all five of his safety belts as he copied what Dev was doing. With a loud SCRUNCH, he kicked a huge padded foot through the roof and down on to the ground.

'The other, too!' Dev said, but Boja was already way ahead of him, kicking through until he was wearing the hut like a huge pair of underpants.

Dev scrambled back up, his energy slowly returning as he pulled out the loose safety belts and bound them together. Then he ran them around Boja like a pair of braces, hoicking the hut under his armpits, while Boja clung on to the outside.

The Hut-On-Wheels had become . . . a Hut-On-Legs.

Suddenly, Pena's nervous fingers slipped from her bowstring, sending a fizzleplop-smeared arrow across the cavern with a loud PSCH-H-H-H-H! As it hit the opposite wall it exploded into pink sparkles, lighting up not just one dark wolf, but several of them.

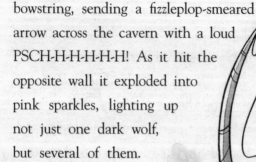

INVENTION 513: The Hut-On-Legs

TUG EACH LIMB

CENTRAL CONTROL BALL

STEER FROM ABOVE

AVERAGE SPEED 207" - MINUS - GROSS WEIGHT °19_Δ = SL15/0°/Δ|| (TOTAL SPEED!)

0"/15 WRAP

SECONDARY GEARS

BOJA ✕✕✕ (NO VERBAL CUES)

BRACE STRAP

MAIN BUCKLES (COMPRESS HUT BY 197°)

BUSTLE

REPURPOSED HANDLE

ANKLE STRAPS

CORE CONTROLS

The sparkles faded. The wolves turned their attention to Pena. Their eyes burned red. Their growling intensified.

'You keep away from her!' Bagby roared, plucking a fistful of fizzleplop bangers from his fur trim and flinging them towards the wolves. They banged, whizzed and popped in a clatter of pink light and confusing noises, as the wolves recoiled into whatever flickering shadows still remained.

'GET IN!' Dev yelled from the hut. Pena was first, grabbing Dev's wrist as he hauled her up. Bagby was next. 'I . . . I got loads more!' he stammered, patting the fizzleplop paste packages behind him. 'I'll throw the whole lot at them if I have to!'

'Nice thought, but you'd bring the cavern down around us,' Santoro muttered, his sword switching from

one wolf to the other as they circled the darkness. Slowly, carefully, he took a few steps back, reaching up his arm as Dev he-e-e-eaved his brother up and inside the hut.

'Well? What's your plan?' Santoro puffed. 'Wait, why's Boja *wearing* the hut?'

'He's going to run us out of here!' Excitement gurgled in Dev's throat as he did up Santoro's safety belt, then clambered on to Boja's back. 'He just needs someone to *drive* him.'

Upon Boja's head lay a small bundle of cords. Once Dev had pulled himself up amongst them he yanked on the nearest, which tightened under Boja's arm, swinging him around like a puppet. As he turned, the hut spun around with him. Boja chuckled. Then Dev gripped another couple of cords, and yanked them together. Boja bellowed like a racehorse, a huge smile across his face as one of his legs lifted off the ground.

The wolves hesitated for a moment.

Then they lunged.

Dev grabbed all of the cords at once and heaved them sharply, sending Boja's feet trotting one, after the other, after the other. The wolves went for his heels, only to get kicked in the face for it. But now Boja was moving. And Dev had no intention of slowing him down. He steered the giggling red bear towards the large crack in the wall – SK-K-K-K-K-K! – as Boja scraped the hut noisily between the rocks before POPPING out the other side.

Back into the moonlit woodlands.

Dev yanked the cords again and Boja sped up, jogging between the long dark shadows of the trees. The hut merrily bobbing up and down as he ran.

'They're not giving up!' Santoro yelled, manning the rear, pointing his sword at the wispy black shapes darting along behind them.

'Well then how about we . . . supercharge?' Dev shouted into Boja's ear.

'SOOPYCHUDGE!' Boja roared. Flember crackled

across his fur. It ran like lightning bolts across his belly, then snaked down, through the holes in the hut roof and around his legs. Flember boots! Bright, glowing *flember boots*!

Boja gripped tighter on to the hut.

Dev gripped tighter on to the cords.

'Let's GO!' Dev cheered, as Boja's strides became longer. Each step bounced a little higher. A little further. Soon Boja was leaping in great arcs across the hollows, the fallen trees, the mossy rocks. As Bagby, Pena and Santoro all shrieked inside the hut, Dev looked down at his big red friend, and they both laughed in utter exhilaration with each and every bound.

'OK,' Santoro yelled. 'To be fair to Boja, this *is* quite impressive.'

Then suddenly, a mistimed jump brought Boja SQUELCH-ing down into some disgustingly thick mud. He leapt again, unable to get much height before sinking back down. The flember around his feet sputtered, faded, buried by the mud as it FRRPP-ed and PARP-ed around them.

Dev looked back to see the wolves weaving through the trees. But when they were only a short distance away, they all stopped.

And they watched.

There was something here they didn't want to get too close to.

'WE'RE SINKING!' Bagby shouted, as FRRP-ing mud billowed up inside the hut. He undid his safety belt, undid Pena's, then both of them clambered up Boja's fur. The mud followed, bubbling around Boja's waist, the hut itself slowly sliding beneath rolling, grassy mounds of sludge.

'No wonder the dark wolves won't follow us here!' Santoro panted, struggling to undo his own belt. 'Dev, we're in a SWAMP!'

'SWAMP!' Boja nervously yelped, his paws clawing at the wet mud, his wide eyes bulging out from their sockets. Panic was taking hold. The mud, clinging heavily on to his fur, was dragging him down.

It was dragging them *all* down.

15

A Sense of Direction

As the mud SQUELCH-ed and PARP-ed its way up Boja's stomach, it pulled the Hut-On-Legs completely out of sight. With it sank Pena's sack of chomptatoes, and Bagby's considerable supply of pink fizzleplop paste. And while most of the passengers were too busy panicking to give either thing much thought, they noticed when the fizzleplop explosions started. Huge air bubbles, BILLOPP-ing out from the mud, bursting into plumes of glittery pink smoke and showering Dev, Santoro, Bagby, Pena and even Boja in a rather delightful layer of sparkles.

Perhaps more importantly, however, the bubbles opened up enough space in the mud for Boja to reach his paws out in front of him, and start to he-e-e-eave himself across the swamp on his belly.

'He's doing it!' Santoro shouted. 'Boja's climbing out from the . . .'

As if he'd spoken too soon, Boja FRRRRP-ed a little deeper back down into the mud. Still, he was not deterred. With a scowl of determination he slapped his paws back out. Flember crackled and sparkled along his arms. Bright, glowing gauntlets formed around his fists. With every ounce of strength he dragged himself forwards, his legs kicking out until his flember could find them too. And then, with an audible FOOSH, his flember boots billowed back into life.

'Well done, Boja!' Dev cheered, gripping a little tighter on to Boja's ears. Now nothing could stop him. Boja pounded the wet mud, propelling himself across the swamp as if a delicious waffle breakfast was waiting on the other side. Dragging not just himself, but all four children on his back.

All four, whooping and cheering, children.

The dark wolves were long out of sight by the time Boja hauled himself into the roots of a wampallo tree. He flumped, exhausted, on to his front, let out a loud 'HOOOOOOOO!' then closed his eyes, instantly drifting off into a deep, satisfied sleep.

A splutter of daisies swayed back and forth in front of his lips.

'That was AMAZING!' Bagby yelled, stepping off Boja's head, on to his nose, and then down on to more solid ground. 'Your bear, it . . . it SAVED us!'

'He's pretty special,' Dev agreed, nudging Santoro.

'Hmmph,' Santoro grumbled.

Pena crouched down, peering close up to Boja's face. 'Maybe Boja isn't so scary after all,' she muttered, jabbing Boja's squishy black nose. 'Dev, did

you . . . did you *summon* him?'

Santoro helped Dev slide down. 'No, I, uh . . . I built him. He's a *robot*.' Bagby and Pena stared, blank-faced. 'Well, I mean, he was made from parts. Like a machine. But flember brought him to life!'

'And then something made him go wrong,' Santoro scowled through his messy, muddy hair.

'He's . . . he's okay,' Dev exclaimed, grabbing fistfuls of sloppy swamp mud and squelching them into Boja's leaf-filled ears. 'As long as he can't hear anything we'll be safe. Then, when we get to Pajoba, maybe I'll be able to fix him properly.'

'I know, I'm on it!' Dev exclaimed, grabbing great fistfuls of sloppy swamp mud and squelching them into Boja's ears. 'This should protect him for now. But I'll need to fix him properly when we get to Pajoba.'

Santoro threw his hands up in the air with frustration. 'IF we do, Dev. Boja is part of the reason we're out here. He *malfunctioned*! He went weird just when we needed him most! And now we're LOST! And we're responsible for two kids who don't know *any* of Nakobe's tricks, you still REFUSE to learn how to defend yourself, and, to come back to my original point, we're absolutely, totally LOST!'

'We're not LOST!' Dev snorted, pulling the backpack

from his shoulder, lifting out the flember book, and opening it up to some of the later pages. 'Nakobe said the elders built their temples along the Flember Stream.' Dev ran the golden F across to one of the triangles on the map. 'I thought Dad was drawing in the high points of the Flember Stream, but maybe he was actually drawing the *temples*. Which means . . . there's another temple . . . all the way over here . . .' He dragged the F across a few more pages. '. . . in PAJOBA! See? We've been following the Flember Stream!'

Santoro stared at him silently for a moment. 'So where . . .' he finally asked '. . . are we *now*?'

'Ah!' Dev flipped back through the pages. 'Well, we hit Dead Drop Canyon, right here. And alongside it, The Grey Woods. Then . . . umm, well we sort of got turned around . . .'

He turned the page on its side. Then upside down. Flipped to the back of it, then looked up, squinting at the moon.

'Huh,' Dev mumbled. 'Where *are* we?'

Santoro slumped down on to the grass, crossed his legs, and buried his face in his hands.

'Anyway, we're not *just* kids,' Bagby protested, having watched the brothers arguing and now folding his arms across his chest.

Pena stood proudly beside him. 'Yeah. We're children of the Wildening. We're VERY powerful.'

'PROVE IT then,' Santoro grumbled.

'We SHOULD prove it!' Dev grinned, planting Elder Nakobe's totem down into the mud. 'Bagby, Pena, we should be using what Nakobe taught us. We should be asking *flember* to guide the way!'

'Let's do it!' Pena cheered, pulling out her totem.

'This time I'm gonna get it right,' Bagby agreed.

The three of them closed their eyes and held out their totems. Dev cleared his mind. He could hear the gentle sounds of the Wildening – the blopping of the swamp, the buzzing of the insects – but soon even that started to fade away. Soon, all he could hear, was . . .

Bagby.

'YARGH!' Bagby yelped. 'NOT AGAIN!'

Dev opened one eye to see the lolloping, graceless shape of Stinkbag the wilderpig bursting through the reeds. It leapt at Bagby with a delighted 'OINK-K-K-K-!', crumpling the boy underneath him as they both splatted into the mud.

'Oink!' Boja mumbled happily in his sleep.

Dev chuckled to himself, then he closed his eyes again.

He could still hear them. Bagby yelling. Pena laughing. Stinkbag oink-oinking. But they were starting to sound more distant. His breathing calmed. His mind was still. And as he sneaked a peek at Elder Nakobe's totem, he could see its lantern was *glowing*.

He opened his eyes wider, excitedly looking down to his feet, hoping to see bright, glowing tree roots.

But there was nothing.

Nothing except cold, squelchy mud around his boots.

'I'm sorry,' he sighed. 'I can't seem to . . .'

Suddenly, he saw movement. Tiny, squirming movement, thin slivers of light wriggling out from the ground. He crouched down for a closer look. 'Ohhh, I remember those things,' Santoro said, crawling alongside. 'We used to catch them out of the rivers in Eden. What were they called, silver something . . .'

'Silverfish,' Dev whispered. His heart started to race. 'I saw them before, under Darkwater, when I was lost in the mines. I saw glowing silverfish just like these and they . . . they guided me towards the *Flember Stream*!'

As he lowered his hand towards them, the silverfish

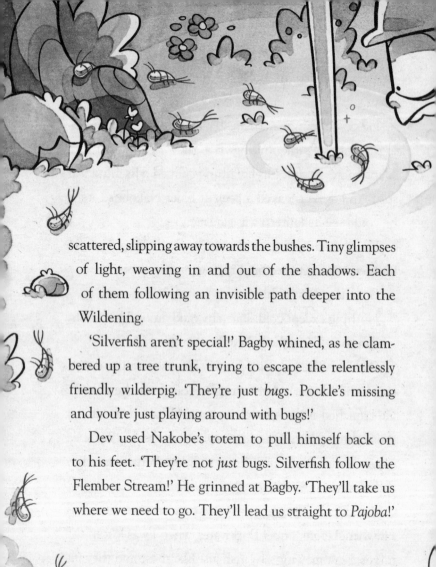

scattered, slipping away towards the bushes. Tiny glimpses of light, weaving in and out of the shadows. Each of them following an invisible path deeper into the Wildening.

'Silverfish aren't special!' Bagby whined, as he clambered up a tree trunk, trying to escape the relentlessly friendly wilderpig. 'They're just *bugs*. Pockle's missing and you're just playing around with bugs!'

Dev used Nakobe's totem to pull himself back on to his feet. 'They're not *just* bugs. Silverfish follow the Flember Stream!' He grinned at Bagby. 'They'll take us where we need to go. They'll lead us straight to *Pajoba*!'

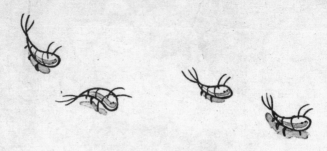

16

The Last Stretch

'SNNCKK! CHOMPTATO!' Boja snorted himself awake. Hovering above his huge, heaving, flember-lit body had amassed a swarm of tiny blinking and flickering lights. Insects. Glowing, sparkling insects. All critters of the Wildening. And while all the buzzing, glowing insects around his head may have been beautiful to see, for this particular sleeping bear they had become a bit annoying.

He rolled to one side and lifted a paw to swat them away.

'Boja, come quickly!' Dev leapt towards him. Boja opened one eye, then lifted a finger to poke the wet mud from his ear. 'No, leave that there for now, Boja.' Dev

shook his head with a smile while grabbing Boja's paw and eagerly pulling the bear up on to his feet. 'Because we're on the move again. We've found it. We've found which way we're going!'

Pena leapt out from a cluster of ferns, Gollup clutched beneath her arm. 'The silverfish are all going this way!' she shouted, pointing deeper into the woods. 'They're moving pretty fast!'

'We can't lose sight of them!' Dev jumped into the ferns and ran past her, just as the last few silverfish slipped away. They slid from the ferns, along the leaves, across roots and around tree trunks. They glimmered against the darkness of the night.

They moved, seemingly, with purpose.

Dev had no idea where on the map they might be

now. The plants were unfamiliar. The flowers were huge. The twisted, knotted trees around the swamp had been replaced by almighty, thick trunks, towering so high into the sky that Dev could barely see where they ended.

Everything felt strange here.

Everything felt a little ominous.

He longed for a moment just to check the flember book, to see if his dad's notes might tell them more about their surroundings. But there was no time. He couldn't afford to lose the trail. He couldn't afford to doubt the silverfish.

Santoro caught up with his brother just as they reached a shallow winding stream. 'Are you sure this is the right way?' he asked. 'Bagby might be right. Silverfish are bugs. We're following *bugs*!'

Dev leapt from rock to rock across the water. 'Elder Nakobe said we're all connected to the Flember Stream,' he said, using her totem to haul himself up the bank on the other side. 'Well, what if she's part of it too now? Just like the Oracle? What if they're both using silverfish to guide us?'

'I'm just saying,' – Santoro stepped across the rocks – 'I preferred it when we were at least following a map.'

Dev paused to catch his breath. 'Now we're following instinct,' he puffed. A smile spread across his face. 'I feel like Elder Nakobe would want us to do that.'

Pena leapt past Santoro, up and on to the bank. 'They're getting away!' she yelled, pointing at the silver-fish slipping between the trees. Dev jumped to attention, and raced alongside her. Santoro was about to follow, only for Bagby to stumble on the slippery rocks beside him, landing face first in the stream.

'HU-U-U-UP!' he gasped, hauling himself back on to his feet. He glanced back, a look of exhausted horror on his face.

'Stinkbag. STINKBAG!'

'OINK!' Stinkbag leapt on to Bagby's back, using him as a stepping stone up and on to the bank. Then he waited, gleefully, for Bagby to follow.

'I can't pick up ANY scent around here,' Bagby whined, cautiously climbing out of the water, his eyes trained on Stinkbag. 'Not with that stinky PIG following me everywhere!'

Then he bolted, as fast as he could, through the woods.

While Stinkbag squealed excitedly after him.

'OINKKKK!' Boja bellowed, leaping the stream in one bound. Stinkbag was chasing Bagby, and Boja was chasing Stinkbag, leaving Santoro to clamber up behind on his own.

'Fine,' Santoro grumbled to himself, as he brushed the mud from his armour. 'Instinct. We're following instinct. Dev is trusting the silverfish, so I will trust Dev.' He hauled himself up the bank. 'But these silverfish had better lead us to Pajoba, otherwise I'm turning us around and we're *all* heading back to Eden.'

The chase, as it had become, led them on for some distance. Down steep hills, along mountainous ridges, through the deepest, darkest corners of the Wildening that Dev had ever seen. Only the fleeting lights of the silverfish kept his heart glowing. And only the rumble of Boja's belly let Dev know that everyone was still following.

Suddenly Pena screeched to a halt. She cocked her head, listening. Dev stopped too, terrified at the thought of what she might be hearing.

'Is it the Skraw?' he asked.

'It's *Pajoba*.' Pena grinned.

The silverfish scattered, disappearing into the hills, but Pena didn't need them any more. She ran on in front of Dev, towards the noise. Towards the *music*. Now Dev could hear it too, a gentle melodic tune echoing across the skies. It led them up a steep, rocky incline, to the very brow of the hill, where they both looked out across the horizon.

A hazy sun shimmered across the waters of what looked like the sea.

Dev saw an enormous walled city, with row upon row of wooden huts all stacked in the foothills.

A long, long line of flickering torches lit the path.

Bagby stepped alongside Dev, and sniffed the nearest tree. 'I recognize the scent!' He beamed.

With a gasp of relief, he flumped down on to his knees. 'We made it HOME!'

Stinkbag slumped down beside him, and nuzzled under his arm.

17

Pajoba

Pajoba was huge, a settlement twice the size of Eden. It too was surrounded by a wall of thick tree trunks,

but its buildings were made from wood, not stone. And they were stacked. Layer upon layer of houses, three, four, five levels high, with walkways and bridges running between them. All of it was built into, and around, the Wildening itself. Toweringly tall trees nestled amongst the cabins, stepped paddies had been carved up by man-made paths, and gentle rivers trickled their way between it all.

Dev, Boja, Santoro and Stinkbag all followed Bagby and Pena through the front gates. Although it was still

early in the morning, everyone was very much awake. The music they had followed came from a small band, each member honking and tooting instruments the like of which Dev had never seen before. Tables had been set out, a long, long line of tables leading all the way along the streets. Crowds of people milled around, some chatting, some carrying chairs, some placing curiously arranged bowls of food down on the tables. Then one by one they fell quiet, as Boja's rumbling stomach loudly announced his arrival.

The big, red, glowing bear lifted a paw, and waved politely. But he wasn't looking at any of them. His eyes were staring longingly at the food on the tables, as if someone might give him permission to slam his face into the middle of it all, and chomp down every last crumb.

'You're back! And just in time for our daily breakfast feast!' A large, very round man in a long, bustling cloak crawled out from under one of the tables. He had big bushy eyebrows and a thin white beard, his face beaming so wide Dev could only see kindness in it. He wiped his hands against his apron, and opened his arms out to hug Bagby and Pena. 'But wait . . . I thought you were training for a few more months! Where's Nakobe?' He caught sight of Gollup, snoozing gently in Pena's arms. 'And where . . . where's *Pockle?*'

Pena's face collapsed into a sob. 'Everything went wrong, Pibbles!' she cried, pressing herself against the man's apron. Bagby, not to be left out, squeezed in beside her.

'Where's Mum?' Bagby whimpered. 'Where's Dad?'

Pibbles stared down at them in stunned silence, then gestured further down the breakfast line. 'They're . . . they're sat at the council tables,' he stammered. 'But why? What happ—'

Neither Bagby nor Pena waited for the end of his sentence. They ran, as fast as they could, in the direction he was pointing, disappearing down the seemingly endless streets. Stinkbag took a moment to snuffle up a few stray berries, then he, too, was gone, urgently oinking after Bagby.

Pibbles turned to Dev, then to Santoro. Then he looked up to the ever-hopeful Boja. 'And who,' he asked, now utterly confused, 'are all of YOU?'

'We, um . . . we've been trying to help Bagby and Pena.' Dev struggled to think of what else to say. His mouth flapped open and closed a few times more. Santoro, too, was struck unusually speechless, and Boja had already stuffed what looked like a giant blue melon inside his mouth.

'We were attacked by the Skraw, you see, and . . .'

Pibbles arched an eyebrow. '*Skraw?*' he replied, taking a step back. He paused for a moment, staring quizzically at Dev. 'Well, *whatever* it was, you should go after Bagby and Pena. Tell the council everything you've seen.'

Dev didn't need to be told twice. With Santoro and Boja close behind, he weaved his way between the towering houses, leaping over chicken crates, potted

plants, all the breakfast-laden carts lining the paths, ducking below huge, elaborate dishes as they were carried over to the tables. Dev spotted what looked like hams, sausages, great racks of ribs. Fruit bowls stacked high with bulging, multicoloured plums. Pastries whipped up into extraordinary shapes, decorated with candied nuts, seeds and jams. Despite Dev's best efforts to prevent Boja's wandering paws, every time he turned around the big, hungry bear had a different type of food stuffed inside his mouth. Usually with someone yelling, waving an empty dish after him.

As the streets of Pajoba started to open up, Dev saw Bagby and Pena head into the more wooded areas. Here the trees grew wide rather than tall, their roots criss-crossing the ground like spiderwebs. Dev, Santoro and Boja struggled to keep up. This was all new ground to them. They tripped, and slipped, and skidded across the dew-soaked grass. They stumbled between the bamboo legs of all the raised wooden huts above them. They fell, many steps at a time, down the tightly woven ladders. And then, finally, they turned one last corner.

Where they saw Bagby and Pena.

'We – puff – we found you!' Dev wheezed, leaning against a moss-rolled boulder. Even though the sun had started to rise over Pajoba, this particular street was a cool, shaded dead end, cast into shadow by the heavily decorated leaves of the trees that surrounded it. Their roots broke up what would have once been a path. A river thick with bright green algae ran through the middle. Still, more tables had been set up along the length of it. More food piled high upon them. More people mingled around.

These people, however, looked rather important.

'What's with all the hats?' Santoro whispered, pointing to the tall green headdresses everyone was wearing. Their robes, too, were stitched in finer detail. Necklaces clinked around their necks. Their hair had been plaited into complicated patterns. And strung from the belts around their waists, Dev noticed they all had their own small totems.

The two elders sitting at the very head of the table looked to be the most important of all. Their hats were tall, like Elder Nakobe's. Their totems were staffs, like Elder Nakobe's.

And, not least of all, Bagby and Pena were hugging them both tightly. Sobbing into their ornate robes.

'Where is your sister?' One of the elders wiped Bagby's tears from his cheeks. She seemed angry, a stern frown pressed between her dark-ringed eyes. 'And *where* is Elder Nakobe?'

Bagby sniffled and snuffled some noises, blew out a few snot bubbles, but he couldn't make any words.

'Elder Pinobei,' the other elder said. He had a gentler way about him, a friendly face creased with wrinkles, and a flock of white hair plaited down his back. 'Whatever happened, they are too upset to tell us. Isn't that right, dear Pena?'

Pena nodded, unable to speak any words either.

So Dev edged nervously towards them all and cleared his throat.

'Um, excuse me,' he said. 'I'm sorry. But Pockle was . . . well, she was *taken*.'

Both elders stared at him in disbelief. Then at Boja, who was discreetly trying to lift an enormous bowl of steamed chomptatoes from the table.

'Taken?' Elder Pinobei demanded.

'The SKRAW,' Santoro added bluntly, finally finding his words. 'Great big thing covered in leaves. It took Pockle. It knocked Elder Nakobe into the crater. It was too strong. Too *fast*.'

Elder Pinobei scowled at mention of the Skraw. 'What do you know of the Skraw? You're not even from the Wildening!' she turned to the friendly-faced elder. 'What do you think of all this, Elder Knuttle?' she demanded.

Ignoring her, Elder Knuttle stroked a hand down his long beard, and eyed the totem in Dev's hands. 'That is not your totem,' he said. 'A totem like that would only belong to someone who truly understood the power of flember.' He held his own totem out. It started to glow. 'You're holding Elder Nakobe's totem.'

142

Santoro stepped forwards, protectively. 'Elder Nakobe didn't survive. And she *gave* Dev her glowing stick, you can ask them. Ask Bagby, ask Pena, they'll tell you.'

Bagby and Pena both looked up from Elder Pinobei's robes, and nodded, snottily. 'She wanted him to have it,' Bagby insisted. 'They've been helping us, Mum. They brought us here. They've looked after us.'

'Elder . . . Nakobe.' Shock washed across Elder Knuttle's face. 'She . . . she's dead?'

'I'm sorry,' Dev stepped forwards. 'We did everything we could. But right now we don't have much time. We need to find Pockle, and I . . . I think we can help you. We know a lot more about the Wildening than you might think . . .'

Elder Pinobei silently lifted her hand to stop him talking. 'Thank you for bringing our children home,' she replied snippily, drawing her robe around them both. 'But the people of Pajoba will take it from here.'

'Please—' Dev started.

'We look after our own,' Elder Knuttle interrupted. 'You three can go home now.'

18

Left Out

'O INK!'

Stinkbag broke the silence, scuttling out from beneath one of the tables with a train of cumbersnatches hanging from his mouth. He looked around, spotted the other diners glaring at him, then slow-w-w-wly slid back into hiding.

Elder Knuttle was the first to stand. On his signal, everyone else at the top tables then stood up and shuffled away, leaving Boja to greedily pick the abandoned food from their plates. They bustled past Dev and Santoro, gathering around the two elders as Elder Pinobei lifted her totem above her head. She closed her eyes. Muttered a few words under her breath. The lantern at the head of the totem started to glow, and as it did, Dev felt a breeze swirl around him. The leaves above started to sway. The branches started to creak.

'Dev,' Santoro whispered. 'What are they . . .'

Suddenly the roots around their feet started to unlock from each other. The thick, twisted trunks of the trees cre-e-e-eaked away. The dead end itself started to split apart, a rustle of leaves parting to reveal quite the most extraordinary sight hidden on the other side.

Another temple.

The one Dev had seen drawn on his map.

This temple looked old, cracked and worn away by the weather, but it stood far more complete than the temple Dev had seen in the pond. This temple was wider. Taller. So tall, in fact, the top half of it was still hidden behind the trees.

Elders Knuttle and Pinobei walked up its broken stone steps, helping Bagby and Pena through the columned archways inside. The rest of the group followed. Stinkbag was quick to chase Bagby, hobbling up the steps with a trail of cumbersnatches dragging behind him, only for a set of two large, metal doors to heave shut in his face.

He snorted, shook his head, then slumped down patiently beside them.

Dev stared for a little while, stunned by what he had

seen. 'They moved the trees!' He stared at the totem in his own hands. 'I summoned a few silverfish but they . . . they moved the *trees!*'

'Whaph going omph?' Boja slurped through a dribbling mouthful of gristle-braised pamplechops. He pointed to the temple. 'Whaph thath?'

'They don't want our help any more,' Santoro huffed. 'We should do what they said, Dev. We should go home.'

'Before you do . . .' The rather round man in an apron, Pibbles, sauntered towards them. He was now carrying his own totem in one hand, and a dish of chippled wharf-nuts, topped with sprinkles, in the other, which he then offered to Dev. 'You should eat. You've had a long journey, I'm sure, and a difficult time keeping Bagby and Pena safe. Can't have you thinking we're entirely ungrateful.'

Dev picked a few wharfnuts, but Santoro reached over

and grabbed a handful. 'At least someone appreciates what we did,' he said, cramming them into his mouth before Boja could even get near.

Pibbles sat down on one of the abandoned chairs. 'There is one thing you should know about the people of the Wildening.' He reached out towards the flember crackling across Boja's fur, allowing it to dance against his fingertip. 'We're suspicious of most outsiders. We don't like them. We don't trust them. We keep away from all but a few of them.'

'Sounds like Eden,' Dev mumbled, before popping some wharfnuts into his mouth. 'We built a big wall too, but we did it to keep the Wildening out.'

'Well we built *ours* to keep outsiders like you out,' Pibbles chuckled. 'It just works best if we keep out of each other's way. Or at least it has done, until now.' Pibbles voice wobbled. He stared at the ground, lost in his own thoughts. Then he coughed, stood, and a polite smile returned to his face. 'They'll be in the temple now. The elders council. All of them discussing what to do next. Talking, arguing, but not actually getting anything done.' He sighed. 'That's what . . . authorities do.'

Dev gulped down one last wharfnut. 'We could help you all find Pockle,' he said. 'We . . . we've come up against the Skraw before, and the dark wolves. I have

Nakobe's totem, Santoro has flember armour, we have a great big BOJA!' He pointed to Boja, who looked up, his cheeks bulging with wharfnuts, his ears still splodged full of swamp mud.

'Well, I mean, he's helpful as long as he can't hear anything.'

Pibbles cast his eye over to Santoro. 'Your brother looks like he'd rather go home,' he smiled. 'Take you and the bear back south, to the mountain, to where you'd be safe, isn't that right?'

'I came out here looking for Dev,' Santoro grumbled. 'I found him. He and Boja found the flember they wanted. I'm sorry for what's happened, but you have a whole city here ready to go looking for Pockle. We have a mum, waiting for us at home. She'll be . . .' Santoro sighed. 'She'll be really worried about us.'

'Of course,' Pibbles nodded. 'Of course. Of course. And your father too I expect.'

'We–' Santoro started.

'Dad died when we were young,' Dev interrupted. He paused for a moment, then pulled the backpack from his shoulder, and slid the flember book out. 'But he wrote this. A book all about flember. And there's a map in it too, a map of the Wildening, a map we've been following all this way!' Dev pressed the glowing F against its pages, lighting up the lines of the map. Following them to the outside wall of Pajoba, and the triangle glowing in the middle of it. 'See? This is where we are now. That's your temple, sitting above the Flember Stream!'

Pibbles stared at the book with wide, glistening eyes.

He looked rather pale.

'Bartle,' he gasped.

'Yes, Bartle!' Dev grinned. 'That was our dad's name!'

'You knew our DAD?' Santoro demanded.

'Of COURSE I knew your father!' Pibbles cheered, grabbing the book and swinging it around as if it was an old friend. 'He

came here many, many, many years ago. Ate like a wilderpig. Particularly partial to my lumpgristle stew, said every mouthful added a few more hairs to his beard. Bartle. Dear, dear Bartle!'

'I *told* you!' Dev gestured towards Santoro. 'This IS Dad's book! He was the Second Pioneer, just like Grace said! He explored the island and he drew it all into this map!'

A smile flickered against Santoro's cheek. 'Huh,' he muttered. 'Maybe it *is* true after all.'

'Well,' Pibbles paused. 'Your dad came this far, at least. But the Flember Stream ends here. Your map, it ends here.' He drew the flember-filled F to the last page, where nothing glowed upon it. 'No more triangles, no more temples, no more anything. I sat with your father, on this very street, and I explained it to him. Pajoba may not be the top of the island, but it is, as far as we know, where the flember runs out.'

'So there's no further to go,' Santoro said.

'Exactly. Your father stayed with us for some weeks, learnt our ways, finished off his map, but then he said he wanted to go home. Back where he belonged. Back up to your mountain.'

Pibbles beamed proudly at both Dev and Santoro. 'And yet here you both are, his sons, his strong, brave sons, having made your way through the Wildening!' He poked Santoro's armour. 'Oh, he would be so pleased with who you have become. Thank you, *thank you*, for allowing me to see what he left to this world.'

He closed the flember book and handed it back to Dev.

'That's really nice and all,' Dev sighed, tucking the book into his backpack. 'But Santoro's right. Pajoba doesn't want us here. Maybe we *should* just go home.'

'Nonsense!' Pibbles pulled up the hood of his cloak. A huge bustling crown of grass, ferns and flowers rode up and wobbled on top of his head. 'They might be the elders, but I'm the *Chief* of Pajoba. And *I* say you're going to help us find Pockle.'

19

Someone Special

'They're Bartle's lads!' Pibbles crashed open the huge temple doors and stormed inside. 'You all must remember Bartle? The outsider! He understood flember as much as any of us, so if they're anything to do with him then I say they can help!'

Dev and Santoro crept in behind. Boja squeezed in too, clonking his head on the doorway before bumping into Dev, who was stood, completely still, staring up at their surroundings.

Gazing in awe at the inside of Pajoba's temple.

The temple was a tall, cavernous space, the walls leaning in as they rose to an astonishing height. It looked like there had been other levels once, even staircases between them, but they had mostly crumbled away, leaving only a few struts poking out from the stonework. Long tapestries hung between them, stopping just short of the doorways, which in turn had been half-buried by fallen columns. It felt cold in here. Dev could see his breath curling out in front of him. In the very centre of the temple, however, was a hazy, glowing light, around which the elders and the council were huddled. Bagby and Pena sat amongst them, smearing the tears from their cheeks.

Stinkbag clearly wasn't concerned about that. He skidded between Pibbles' legs, raced across the cobbled stone floor, leapt up at Bagby, and toppled him over in a flurry of excited oinks. Bagby shouted out a few noises in despair.

Elder Pinobei leant out from the huddle. 'I don't care who they are, Pibbles, they're outsiders! Outsiders bring trouble with them.'

'Mum, please!' Pena tugged on her robes. 'They helped us!'

Pibbles strode purposefully towards the elders. 'I may spend my days working on the breakfast menus, because I love it, and I *really* do love it, but my *duty* is the safety of this citadel, and everyone inside it. THAT one,' he swung a pointed finger towards a rather nervous Dev. 'He has Nakobe's totem. He has a book full of Bartle's work.

His brother's wearing some kind of glowing armour. His BEAR is . . .'

Boja rubbed his forehead, grumbled, and then farted.

'Well, I don't know what his bear is. But my point remains. They already know more about flember than you might like to admit. So they can help us find *Pockle!*'

Elder Pinobei muttered curses under her breath, but Elder Knuttle leant in towards her. 'If what Bagby and Pena say is true, Elder Nakobe *did* entrust the boy with her totem.' He shrugged. 'She must have seen something special in him.'

'Well, what, exactly,' Elder Pinobei snapped, 'would you have him *do?*'

'Dev's going to perform a Flemble Ceremony!' Pibbles said with a cheer, hustling the council members on to their feet. As they stepped back, Dev saw they had been gathered around a large circular grate in the stone floor. It was scattered with dried flowers. A gently glowing smoke trailed out. One council member had been sitting beside it, breathing deeply, their glazed eyes staring off into space. Another member now led them carefully away.

'As you can see, we were performing the ceremony before you came in,' Elder Pinobei's voice began to rise in annoyance. 'We followed the Flember Stream as far as we could. There's no sign of Pockle. Nothing!'

A very cold feeling prickled across Dev's skin. 'Wait, what is a *Flemble Ceremony*?'

'It is how we connect to the Flember Stream.' Pibbles beckoned Dev to sit down, not beside the grate, but on top of it.

The smoke wafted up and around him.

It felt warm.

It felt *healing*.

'And sometimes, when we do connect,' Pibbles continued, 'we can see further than we might ever have thought possible. We can see what else is happening across the island.'

'Just like the *Oracle*,' Dev gasped.

Elders Pinobei and Knuttle glanced at each other.

'He knows the Oracle,' Elder Knuttle whispered.

'He knows a lot!' Pibbles said. 'I told you!'

'Dev can summon too!' Pena added proudly. 'We saw it in the meadow! He got it first time! Then again, with the silverfish, they led us right here!'

Pibbles clapped his hands together in delight. 'There you go, there you GO! The more I learn about this lad,

157

the more I *know* he's our best chance of finding Pockle.'

Dev clutched Nakobe's totem tightly. He could feel the rest of the council watching him, and it was making him nervous.

'What . . . what do I do?' he asked.

'Well, you already know from your map that our temples lie along the Flember Stream.' Pibbles fussed around adding some more dried flowers around Dev's legs. 'Our temple isn't quite close enough to reach it, but we can still reap its rewards. We get the smoke, the vapour. Like sitting by a fire and basking in its heat. We experience the Flember Stream not by its flember, but by the trace it leaves behind.'

Dev peered between the holes in the grate. The faintest of glows shimmered up through the darkness, a glow he could only just see if he really, really squinted.

'That's the Flember Stream?' he asked.

'Yes it is,' Pibbles replied. 'Now close your eyes, clear your mind, and let it lead you towards Pockle.'

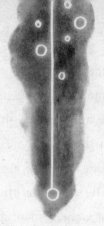

20

The Flemble Ceremony

Dev shot one last glance to a rather bemused Santoro and Boja, then did as he was told. He closed his eyes. His body started to relax. His hearing sharpened. He could hear the tentative shuffling of the council behind him. An annoyed huff of air through Elder Pinobei's flaring nostrils. An occasional slight cough echoing around the temple.

And then the sounds faded away. His head started to feel a bit woozy. His thoughts became confused. Foggy. His body, too, felt a lot lighter, almost as if he might be floating above the ground.

His pulse slowed.

His own breathing echoed loudly inside his ears.

Everything became calm.

Everything became peaceful.

Then there came a new sound. It was very quiet, as if it were far, far in the distance. A bird, chirping. A few birds chirping. But he wasn't just hearing the birds. It was almost as if he could *feel* the noises they were making. As if he just knew, somewhere, that these birds were chirping.

It felt a little unsettling.

Then he felt another sound. Rumbling. Hooves! It sounded like . . . like wilderbuffalo cantering across a plain. Water. Trickling water. Somewhere further south. Then laughter. It came from the east. Somehow, somewhere, he could feel someone was laughing at their own joke. Someone he didn't know. Somewhere he'd never been. But prickling through every inch of his body, of his flember, he could just *feel* it.

And then it occurred to Dev just what was happening.

I'm connecting to the island, he thought. *Just like the Oracle. Just like Nakobe. I'm listening to its flember. I'm feeling . . . everything that's happening!*

More talking. The buzzing of bees. The almighty crash of a tree toppling to the ground. The doompf-doompf-doompf of a heart. Dev could feel it all. And as it grew in volume,

small glimmers of light started to
dance behind Dev's eyelids. Tiny, faint sparks.
Each one pulsing to a different sound. They merged,
then blinked out of existence completely, before more
plink-plink-plinked to fill the space.

And now I can see it, too.

A voice crept in through the glimmering blur of
lights. 'Can you see her?' Pibbles whispered. 'Dev, look
for Pockle. Look for her *flember*.'

Dev tried moving the lights around. Passing them
from one side of his vision to the other, as if he was
wading across the island itself. Feeling every sound.
Searching every nook and crevice of the island. Trying
to find any sign of Pockle, wherever the Skraw might
have taken her.

And then, all of a sudden, he could feel nothing at all.

He had crossed what seemed to be a boundary, beyond
which the glimmers of flember blinked away. He could
feel no sound here. No noise. Just a great long stretch
of darkness, with the thinnest of glowing lines running
through it.

Dev suddenly felt quite alone. He felt cold.

Then the line ran out.

A few solitary lights glowed at its end. They hovered
in a circle, shimmering like stars in an empty night sky.

Dev tried to focus on them, tried to get as close as he possibly could.

'Pockle,' Dev whispered. 'Pockle, are you there?'

'*Found* me!' Pockle's voice giggled back.

Suddenly, another light blinked amongst them. A red light. This one glowed brighter then the others, and as soon as it appeared, it started racing through Dev's mind. Down, across the darkness, cutting a swathe through the lights below. Travelling so fast he could barely keep up with it. It was determined. It felt . . . *hungry*.

Instantly Dev felt himself being dragged away, away from the lights, away from all the sounds, the feelings, and back into the cold main hall of the temple. He let out a loud 'GASPPP!' as he jolted awake. His heart pounded. His skin was clammy. Pibbles grabbed his shoulders, trying to hold onto him, but Dev wouldn't keep still.

'I found Pockle! She's OK,' Dev muttered. 'But it's coming! It's COMING!'

'What's coming Dev? What is it?'

Dev span around and stared Pibbles right in the eye.

'THE SKRAW!' he cried. 'THE SKRAW IS COMING HERE!'

21

Return of the Skraw

'Bring it on.' Santoro grinned, pulling out his sword. His armour started to light up with flember. 'Whatever the Skraw is, this time we'll be ready for it!'

'Skraw! Again they talk of the SKRAW!' Elder Pinobei threw her hands up in dismay. 'There is no Skraw! This boy has seen nothing!'

Dev was already on his feet, standing by the open doors of the temple. He stared into the soft pink hues of the early morning sky. Then he saw it. The ragged shape of the Skraw plummeting through the clouds. Its wings tucked into its body as it crashed beyond the trees. Its jarring, rattling music echoed across Pajoba. A cry went up. The sound of wailing. Of crashing. Of things being

torn apart.

'Whatever it is,' Pibbles scowled from beside him. 'It made the wrong decision interrupting our BREAKFAST!' He swung around to the other elders. 'Protect the temple,' he barked. 'Protect the Flember Stream!'

'Now hang on . . .' Elder Knuttle protested.

Pibbles wasn't listening. He marched through the open doors, nodding to Dev as he passed.

'You say you've seen the Skraw before,' he said. 'Well then I could do with your help.'

Dev looked back to Santoro, who angrily swung his

sword towards a rather alarmed-looking Boja. 'You're not going out there!' Santoro growled. 'You saw what happened last time that . . . that *thing* turned up. What if Boja gets all angry again?'

'HELLO?' Boja boomed, unaware his voice was coming out as loud as it was.

Dev thought for a moment, carefully considering his options. 'Boja has mud in his ears, so he shouldn't be able to hear the music,' he said. 'You'll be safer in here with him. You all will. You can protect him, protect his flember. I . . . well, maybe I can help catch the Skraw!'

'Catch it HOW?' Santoro called out, but the temple doors were already closing. Pibbles was already gone.

And Dev was racing after him.

'The Skraw tries to take *flember*!' Dev puffed, following Pibbles as they headed towards the music. 'It can't hold it, but it tries. It has these . . . these *tendrils* which sink into the ground. We'll have to be careful. It's really powerful.'

'I've heard of the Skraw.' Pibbles frowned. 'But there's only one of it, and there are *many* of us.'

He lifted his totem above his head. It started to glow and, as it did, Dev noticed movement around them. Shadows slipped out from the trees, from the ground, blurring through the rustling ferns. Dev squinted. They were *people*! People running alongside them. They looked strong and determined. They wore outfits made of woven

green leather, strapped by vines and decorated with long grass. They moved silently. Gracefully. Quickly. Flanking Dev and Pibbles. Each holding out a small, glowing totem of their own.

'Soldiers of the flember!' Pibbles beamed proudly. 'They're some way off becoming elders, but they're learning. They've studied flember for years. Even your dad trained with them for a . . . '

His voice faltered. They had reached the main streets of Pajoba, and everything ahead of them was carnage. The Skraw had landed in a nest of three-tiered huts and torn a devastating gash through the length of them. It crouched in the remains of the ground floor, its torn cloak of leaves spinning around, its long beak snapping at anyone who came too close. All those who had been enjoying breakfast formed a mob, clutching whatever they could find as weapons. Chairs. Branches. Legs of ham.

'I didn't imagine the Skraw would look like *this*,' Pibbles gasped, as Dev stepped up behind him.

The Skraw lurched forwards, its thick black claws tearing up the ground. The mob swayed back. This close, the music was almost deafening. 'BE CAREFUL!' Pibbles yelled, gesturing the flember soldiers forwards. 'The Skraw will try to take your flember, so use *everything* around you!'

The soldiers charged, their glowing totems seemingly lifting the ground from beneath their feet. Grass billowed up like a wave. It carried them through the crowd, as vines swung down from the trees and lifted them higher, before peppering them down upon the Skraw.

The Skraw, however, stood fast. Bright red flember crackled round its body like a shell, whipping the soldiers away, while its tendrils sank into the blossoming surroundings. And swiftly those surroundings started to die. The grass crinkled, the trees wilted, the leaves fell. The flember soldiers had little to grip on to.

'This is what I saw before!' Dev shouted to Pibbles. 'You can't use flember against the Skraw!'

The crowd started to back away. The dying patches of ground had panicked them. Some started to flee. The soldiers battled on, but the Skraw was too frenzied, too wild, to let any of them get close.

'Then what . . . ?' A rather pale Pibbles stared at the Skraw. 'What are we supposed to do?'

'I need *chickens*!' Dev replied. He turned Pibbles to face him, and then spoke slowly and carefully. 'Pibbles, I can trap the Skraw. But I'm going to need *chickens*.'

22

Chickens!

'Chickens. Yes, of course,' Pibbles muttered. 'Your father's ideas could be a little random, too. But, somehow, they always seemed to work out.' He led Dev to the house of a woman named Larago, the best chicken wrangler in Pajoba. She, however, was just as terrified as everyone else, and was currently sitting on her own roof, hiding behind a stack of barrels. Her chickens had once been in a line of stacked cages outside, but the commotion and panic had crushed the wood and netting and set them all free. Now the chickens wandered aimlessly across the street: squawking, and flapping, and laying the occasional egg.

'Hang on,' Pibbles finally said. 'Why do you need

chickens?'

'I'm a bit of an inventor.' Dev beamed. He picked
up a few bits of broken cage, bending and twisting and
shaping the pieces around each other. 'It's how I solve
things. How I *fix* things.' He borrowed a couple of barrels,
strung them on top, then found a length of netting hanging between Larago's house and the next, plucked off the
jackfruit jerky that had been drying upon it, and strapped
it all together.

'So if we can't use flember to bring the Skraw down,

INVENTION 514: Double-Barrelled Chicken Cannon

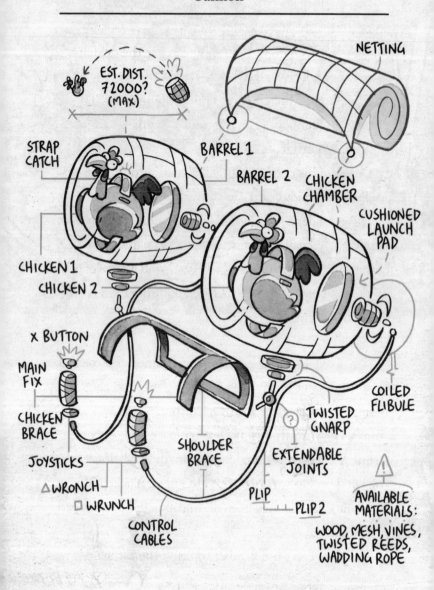

EST. DIST. 72000? (MAX)

NETTING

STRAP CATCH

BARREL 1

BARREL 2

CHICKEN CHAMBER

CUSHIONED LAUNCH PAD

CHICKEN 1

CHICKEN 2

X BUTTON

MAIN FIX

CHICKEN BRACE

JOYSTICKS

△ WRONCH

□ WRUNCH

SHOULDER BRACE

CONTROL CABLES

COILED FLIBULE

TWISTED GNARP

EXTENDABLE JOINTS

PLIP

PLIP 2

⚠ AVAILABLE MATERIALS:

WOOD, MESH, VINES, TWISTED REEDS, WADDING ROPE

then I'll use my own ideas.'

Dev hauled the Double-Barrelled Chicken Cannon up on to his shoulder, and flexed his fingers around the triggers. 'HEY, SKRAW!' he shouted over the deafening music. 'TELL US WHERE POCKLE IS!'

The Skraw, who had only just disentangled itself from a destroyed canopy, swung around towards Dev. A red glow burned inside its eyes.

Dev held his nerve, digging his heels into the ground.

'I'm not afraid of you,' he growled.

His confidence shattered, however, as soon as the Skraw started galloping towards him. In panic he pulled both triggers. With a loud BU-KAWK, and a huge explosion of feathers, a chicken rocketed out from each barrel, the net billowing out behind them.

Only for the Skraw to duck underneath it.

'Oh but I planned for *this*.' Dev grinned. He reached into his pocket and pulled out a fistful of chicken seed he'd scooped from the cages. 'WHAT ARE THEIR NAMES?'

Larago peered down from her rooftop. 'Chooks?' She shrugged.

Dev threw the seed up above his head. 'HERE, CHOOK, CHOOK CHOOK CHOOK!'

The chickens, suddenly hypnotized by the call of food, pulled a sharp right in mid-air. The net swished behind them and swooped down upon the Skraw, slamming it face first into the ground as it skidded towards Dev's boots.

'It WORKED!' Pibbles, who had built himself some armour out of wooden serving dishes while Dev made his cannon, leapt with joy. 'Dev, you CAUGHT it!'

'It DID work!' Dev quickly grabbed the ends of the net, scooping it into a bundle so he could hold it closed. 'To be honest, I'm as surprised as you.'

The Skraw's bony arms thrashed around inside, its wings straining to break through the cords. Its tendrils snaked perilously close towards Dev's face. Both Dev and Pibbles tried their hardest to hold it down, but the Skraw was too strong. It slowly rose up on to its thin legs. Its

cloak shuffled down its body. A cold breath snorted out
from its beak.

A furious red light ebbed from between its ribs.

Dev gulped nervously.

Suddenly the Skraw spun around, dragging the net
behind it. Pibbles lost his hold, but Dev held on. The
Skraw bolted through the streets, swerving left, then
right, rolling him against the walls, smashing him across
the wreckage, but Dev still gripped the net tightly – even
as the Skraw's black, broken wings finally broke through,
stretched to their full length, and hauled them both off
the ground.

The huge city of Pajoba spun dizzily below Dev's feet.

Still he held on.

His stomach lurching up into his throat.

As quickly as they had risen, however, they then started to fall, as the Skraw spiralled back down towards the treetops. But Dev soon realized it wasn't the trees that the Skraw was aiming for.

It was the temple hidden behind them.

Together they tore through a canopy of leaves, crashing through the huge metal doors with an almighty CLANG-G-G-G! and then rolling wildly along the hard stone floor. When Dev finally let go, his exhausted body was left to roll a little bit further, before headbutting into Boja's ample bottom.

He staggered to his feet, clutching his head, partly to steady himself, partly to try and stop the incessant pounding of the music.

He reached out and clung on to Boja's fur for balance.

And then he looked up.

Straight into Boja's glowing red eyes.

23

The Steal

Boja let out a roar so loud it shook the dust from between every brick of the temple. His fur bristled. His teeth glistened. His bright red flember crackled loudly around him. Before anyone had time to react, the bear suddenly wrapped his huge paws around Dev, sque-e-e-ezing him, lifting his feet clean off the ground.

'Boja, stop!' Dev writhed. 'Put me down!'

He could see the swamp mud crumbling from Boja's ears. 'It's been *drying out!*' he gasped. 'Boja's hearing the music

just like before!'

Santoro swung his sword towards the bear, slicing a clump of fur from one of his big red buttocks. Boja yelped. His grip loosened. Dev slid out, stumbling on to the ground as Boja snapped around towards Santoro, his lip curled into a spit-dripping snarl.

And then, Boja's big black nose twitched.

He had caught a scent.

He turned towards the small crowd huddled in the centre of the temple, frowned, and started to STOMP-STOMP-STOMP towards them. Elder Pinobei and Elder Knuttle stood defiantly in front of him, totems shining. But Boja wasn't interested in any of them. Instead his eyes were locked on the grate in the ground, and the delicate wisps of flember smoke rising up from below.

'Flem . . . buhhh,' Boja murmured, slamming his face into the grate, and desperately clawing at the stonework around it.

Bagby stepped out in front of his parents. 'Stand back everyone!' he proudly declared, reaching into his cloak and pulling out his last few fizzleplop bangers. 'We've faced this monster before, but this time I'm ready for him!'

Boja lifted his head, snarled, and let out the most bone-shaking, temple-rattling roar any of them had ever heard. It sent Bagby skidding back in a drizzle of spit. In shock, he dropped the bangers, which exploded around his feet in a noisy plume of pink sparkles. While Pena helped Bagby back on to his feet, Stinkbag rushed forwards, growling defensively at Boja. Boja stared at the little wilderpig through red, glowing eyes, sniffed, then returned to clawing at the ground.

'Flember,' Dev muttered to himself. 'Boja's . . . trying to get more *flember*.'

'DEV!' Santoro yelled, pointing his sword to the shredded netting on the floor. Dev's blood ran cold. The Skraw had *gone*. He looked around frantically, then up, into the shadowy heights of the temple, trying to catch sight of where it might be hiding, only for its thick claws to slam down upon him from behind. He crumpled to the ground, pinned, the wind knocked out of his lungs and the Skraw's music pounding so loudly in his ears that he could barely hear himself think. As he struggled to break free, he twisted around just in time to see his brother leaping towards them.

Sword drawn.

Santoro sliced clean through one of the Skraw's arms.

The Skraw snapped its neck back with a bellow.

Its arm fell to the ground, releasing its hold on Dev, but then it swung its other claw around Santoro's waist, swooping its leafy cape around him as if it were swallowing him whole. Santoro tried to pull his sword back but his arms were too tightly clamped against his sides. He yelled, but the sound was lost against the music, the Skraw's wings opened out and – WOOOSHHH – it barrelled them both back out through the main door, ricocheting from tree trunk to tree trunk and then up, into the cloudy skies.

Dev tried to call out his brother's name, but he had no breath left to do it. His pulse hammered loudly in his ears. His arms were wobbly, his legs even wobblier. The music was still playing. Not as loudly, but he could still hear it. The *arm*. It was coming from the Skraw's severed *arm*. Quickly he stamped the heel of his boot against it, over and over, crunching the music into beeps and squawks.

And then, eventually, silence.

A commotion rose behind Dev. Words, blurring together. He turned to see Bagby trying to get his attention, waggling his hitting stick towards a very frazzled-looking Boja.

The bear's flember had calmed from red back to

normal. His bulging eyes looked nervously around the room. He tried to pat the dust and rubble back into the ground, then FLOMP-ed down on to his bottom, then FLOMP-ed on to his back. His eyes started spinning inside their sockets. 'Very . . .' he puffed, his whole stomach heaving with every breath. 'So-rry . . . soh . . . ssss . . .'

Then with a hiccup from one end, and a fart from the other, Boja's eyes closed shut, and he sank into an exhausted sleep.

'Boja, NO!' Dev climbed to his feet and staggered towards the bear. 'Boja I need you awake. We have to find Santoro. The Skraw *took* Santoro!' His voice faltered. He stroked Boja's chest fur, and as it parted he saw there, on Boja's synthetic skin, a black mark, just like the one on the side of his tongue. But this mark was larger. It had spread further. And it bulged, like a line of rocks.

'It has come back,' Pibbles said shakily as he stood beside Dev, the rest of the council hesitantly moving to surround them.

Dev looked to them all for answers. 'What? What has come back?' he cried. 'What's happening to Boja? Please, please tell me!'

'It would be quicker if we showed you,' Pibbles said.

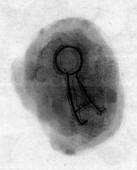

24

A Warning

At Pibbles' call, a select few members of the council stepped forward. They were dressed slightly differently from the others – their clothes were shabbier, their necks decorated by roll upon roll of beaded necklaces. They cautiously made their way towards Boja, then started waving their own glowing totems across him. These, Pibbles explained, were some of the finest flember doctors in Pajoba. Although they might not have encountered marks quite like this before, they would encourage Boja's own flember to heal him.

For the moment, at least, he would be well looked after.

Pibbles then beckoned Dev over to the temple wall, where he gripped one of its tapestries by the corner. He yanked it hard, pulling it ping-ping-ping from its fastenings, as it billowed down on to the ground.

Then he held his totem out, and pressed its lantern against the wall.

'Our ancestors carved their stories into their temples,' he said, as Dev edged closer. He could see them now, faint scratches in the stone, shapes, maybe, although they were too weathered to make out. 'And we hid them, so only those who truly understand flember might ever be able to see.'

His totem started to glow. As it did, tiny lights glimmered around it. Tiny, sparkling lights, which danced across the walls, slipping into the notches, the scratches, lighting up a line of carvings as if they had been etched in starlight.

'Flemberthyst crystals,' Dev gasped, running his finger gently down the lines as the glowing dust trailed behind it. 'Crushed and painted in. Just like the map inside my book. Completely invisible until someone passes flember along it.'

'Told you,' Pibbles nodded back towards Elders Pinobei and Knuttle. 'The boy knows his stuff.'

The two elders grumbled as they, and the rest of the

council, came over and huddled around the carvings. Bagby and Pena squee-e-e-ezed in between.

'Whoa!' Bagby stared up at the glowing carvings. 'That's so COOL!'

Pena held Gollup up for a closer look. Gollup golluped, then slowly drifted back to sleep. 'What does it say?' Pena asked, excitedly. 'What does it all MEAN?'

'I think I can work it out,' Dev said, stepping back to read the highest carvings.

'Is this . . . is this Flember Island?'
Dev asked, pointing at the wall. 'There
are so many animals here I don't
recognize.'

'*Injay jototay*,' Elder Pinobei said. 'Not just animals. Hills. Mountains. Trees. *Dohan*.'

'Dohan!' Bagby cheered triumphantly, turning to his sister. 'I told you. I TOLD you! The Dohan are real!'

'What *are* they?' Dev asked.

Pena rolled her eyes. 'They were supposed to be like mountains,' she replied. 'Literally, mountains. Great big chunks of Flember Island itself. And they were, well, they were alive. As in, they could get up and walk around. That was the legend, anyway. But *most* of us grew out of believing it.'

Bagby snorted. 'It's said the Dohan had their flember taken away, so now they just lie around doing nothing. Well, when I can summon flember, I'm going to RAISE a Dohan back up. Then you'll see. Then you'll all be THANKING me.'

'SHHH!' Elder Pinobei hushed him down. Then she reached up and rolled her own totem across the carvings. The glowing lines of flember followed, resting upon a row of figures beneath the Dohan.

'Elders,' she said, with a sadness in her voice.

Elder Knuttle stepped forward, nudging her totem across to the next carving. A figure formed amongst the lines.

A monstrous, scratchy, terrifying figure.

Dev leant closer. 'Is that . . . the Skraw?' he asked.

'The Skraw steals flember. It controls it. Uses it for evil,' Elder Knuttle said. 'The Skraw carved here came to our island many, many years ago, *hundreds* of years ago, and did just that. It tried to turn the island against itself, it hurt a great many of the elders, but eventually, it was defeated. Our ancestors cast its body to the very ends of the island. Then they turned the earth so the Flember Stream might never reach it. So it might never know flember again.'

Pibbles scowled at the carvings. 'And yet somehow,'

he said, 'the Skraw seems to have come back.'

'I saw a place where the Flember Stream ran out,' Dev gasped. 'In the Flemble Ceremony. I saw a place that was so dark, only a few lights shone there.'

The elders all looked at each other with a fear in their eyes.

'You saw . . . the *Deadlands*?' Pibbles asked.

'We would never think to look in the Deadlands,' Elder Pinobei muttered. 'Why would we? There's nothing *there*!'

'It's where the Skraw came from!' Dev cried. 'I saw Pockle there, I *heard* her, so it will have taken Santoro there too! We have to go! We have to . . .' He glanced over to Boja – poor, wheezing Boja, still asleep on the temple floor while the doctors hovered around him. 'I . . . I'll need Boja to come with me though.'

Boja raised a finger of his paw from the ground. 'After . . . breakfascht,' he mumbled.

'Dev, this is exactly what we're trying to show you,' Pibbles insisted. 'Look. Right here. Look what is happening!'

'To turn someone's flember red is to *control* them,' Pibbles explained. 'When the Skraw first attacked our island, it tried to do just that. And, although it was defeated, all the things it had touched were left with the

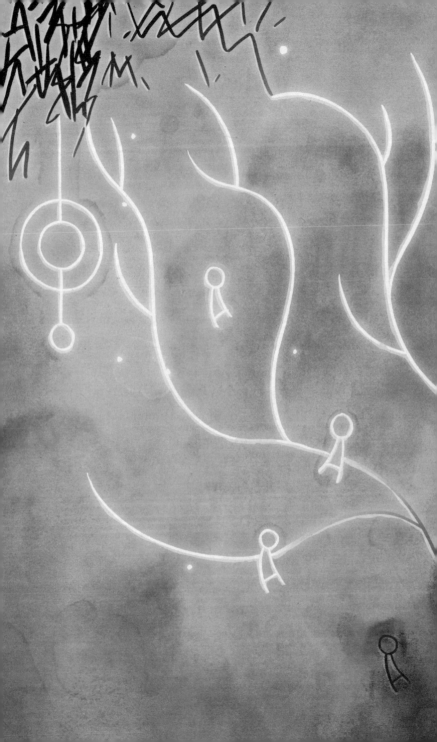

consequences.'

The glowing lines converged towards a few figures. No light shone out from them. No flember.

'Red flember leaves behind a *poison*,' Pibbles whispered. 'Dev, every time the Skraw controls Boja, it is *poisoning* his body.'

25

The Shore

Lesson over, the elders were not hanging around. Pibbles led Knuttle and Pinobei through the main doors and down the temple steps, then hurried them into Pajoba's heavily wooded lowlands. Dev was expected to stay with Boja but, with the bear in the care of the doctors, he had too many questions to just stay put. He raced down the temple steps, frantically trying to catch their attention.

'Wait!' he cried. 'Where are you all going?'

Pibbles didn't slow down. 'You said it yourself,' he puffed. 'The Skraw is hiding in the Deadlands. It has Pockle. It has your brother. If we're to put an end to this, we must go there now!'

'Then I'm coming with you!'

Elder Pinobei shuffled in front of him, stopping him in his tracks. 'What about your bear?'

'He . . . he'll be OK,' Dev said, not entirely sure himself. 'I mean, he'll get better, right? And when he does, we can come with you.'

Pibbles finally stopped. There was an unusual sternness in his voice. 'Dev, the Deadlands are forbidden. They're forbidden to us, and they're especially forbidden to outsiders. There's no way we could let you come with us. No way at all.'

'But . . . but Santoro . . .' Dev pleaded.

'We'll bring him back,' Pibbles insisted, lifting his totem high above his head. 'We're not going alone, you know. We're taking a whole *army*.'

He started walking again, his totem glowing above him. Suddenly Dev noticed flember soldiers emerging from the trees. They slinked through the shadows, trailing behind the elders, their own totems clinking against their belts. Within moments, a huge swathe of them had amassed along the path, all marching into the lowlands. Between the looming boulders, the bowing trees, gathering just below a huge wall of vine-strapped tree trunks.

'Wait! WAIT!' Dev puffed, slipping through their ranks as he struggled to keep up. 'This is a bad idea! You

tried to fight the Skraw before and it didn't work. I've seen the Deadlands. I saw the Flember Stream end there, but it's so faint, so weak, nothing could grow above it. You won't find flember. Your totems won't even *work*!'

Elder Pinobei caught Dev's eye. Her usual stern expression had softened a little. The tiniest of smiles flittered across her lips. 'Flember finds a way. Flember *always* finds a way. If we are to save Pockle, a child of the Wildening, then flember will help us do that.'

'Whatever the odds,' Elder Knuttle agreed. 'We have to believe.'

He lifted his totem a little higher, then closed his eyes. Pinobei did the same. Both their totems started to glow as a familiar warm breeze ran across Dev's skin. The leaves of the trees started to rustle, the grass started to sway. The branches hanging down around them started to cre-e-eak. Dev could feel the soft ground moving beneath his boots. He could see the trees start to lean. Then, with a loud splintering noise, the wall of tree trunks before him split apart. Vines snapped, the soil turned, as two large doors opened up, revealing a sight beyond that struck fear into Dev's heart.

The sea.

'Get away! Those waters *burn*!' Dev stepped back. 'I've seen it. I've been to Darkwater. The sea is not a safe place for anyone!'

'This isn't the sea,' Pibbles chuckled, walking through the gates on to a soft, muddy shoreline. 'The Deadlands lie beyond a lake so huge you cannot see its edges. But it is *clean* water all the way. You see?' He lifted his robes to reveal two sandalled feet, then he stepped into the lapping waves and started splashing about. 'It is untouched by the sea's poisons!'

Then he caught sight of Dev's nervous expression, and he put his serious face back on.

'Dev, you believe in flember, I know you do.' Pibbles splashed out of the water, and rested his hands on Dev's shoulders. 'But you've been through so much. You've lost your brother, your bear is unwell, your faith in flember must be sorely tested.'

Dev could feel tears welling in his eyes, but he refused to let them out.

'So, in the meantime, put your faith in *us*.' Pibbles smiled.

Dev looked around at the other elders gathered on the shore. They were pointing their totems, directing some of the flember soldiers towards the lowest hanging branches. These were then snapped off, while other soldiers set to binding them together with reeds. The creaks, and cracks, and shouts between them all sounded busy, organized, like a workforce.

'But I . . . I can help you.' Dev sniffed. 'I'm . . .'

'A brilliant inventor, I know.' Pibbles patted him on the back and turned him back towards the path. 'But we have an awful lot of rafts to build, and not a lot of time. So right now, you would be better placed back in the temple, tending to your friend Boja.'

Dev sighed, and reluctantly started the long walk back.

'We'll be fine, Dev!' Pibbles called after him. 'Flember always finds a way!'

26

An Alternative Plan

'I'm OH-KAYYYYYY!' Boja boomed, bursting out through the temple doors and sending a flurry of doctors scattering around him. He stumbled, then slid down each step, staggering on to the path, instantly losing his balance before crashing into an elegant display of pots opposite. 'OH-KAYYYY!' he gurgled, snorting soil out from his nose.

'Boja!' Dev rushed towards the bear. He rested a hand on his belly, brushing his fur, looking for the black marks along his side. But they were faded. Almost invisible.

A bundle of emotions swelled up into Dev's heart as he turned to the bedraggled flember doctors. 'You . . . fixed him?' He beamed. 'You got rid of the poison?'

One doctor, the most senior-looking of them all, readjusted her hat and brushed down her cloaks. 'My name is Doctor Jhunto.' She bowed, gracefully. 'Your bear's body is unlike anything we have encountered before. We encourage our patients' own flember to heal them, it can take hours, days, even weeks. But his body worked so *quickly*!'

Dev helped Boja back on to his feet, then flung his arms around the bear's stomach. 'There are some finely tuned engine parts in here,' he sobbed, tears finally spilling from his eyes. 'Boja, I'm so glad you're OK!'

The doctor cleared her throat. 'He must, however, be . . . *careful*,' she added. 'A poison like that grows. It spreads. If his flember is turned red again, the poison might spread even further, and then it will be harder to fight.'

'I'll keep him safe,' Dev insisted, hugging Boja even tighter. 'Maybe . . . maybe I can invent giant ear muffs, to protect Boja from the Skraw's music, or . . . or I can make something even noisier, to drown it out!'

Boja wrapped his big arms around Dev, squeezing him until there was barely a breath left in his body. 'Schleepy . . .' Boja slurred.

Dev slipped out from Boja's grip, gasped some air back into his lungs, then poked the bear awake. 'Not yet,' he said. 'Boja, we still have SO MUCH to do!'

'Well, then. What's the PLAN?' Bagby yelled, leaping down the temple steps two at a time. Stinkbag followed, eventually rolling under Bagby's legs and sending him crashing down into Boja's furry backside.

Bagby yelled grumpily.

Stinkbag oinked gleefully.

Pena walked out with a little more grace, the snoozing, glowing Gollup still tucked under her arm. 'Are the elders going to find the Skraw?' she asked. 'Are they going to bring Pockle and Santoro back?'

Dev noticed the doctors still loitering, their heads tilted, as they pretended not to be listening. He ushered Bagby and Pena away, and he lowered his voice. 'They said they're going to try,' he whispered. 'But there's no flember in the Deadlands. When they get there, they'll be powerless!'

'So we'll go help!' Bagby grinned, clutching his hitting stick. Stinkbag oinked in agreement.

'They told me to stay here,' Dev sighed. 'They're busy building rafts now, but that's going to take them ages, and they wouldn't even let me help with that!'

Pena tucked in even closer. 'We might still be learning about flember, but one thing's always been very, *very* obvious.' She cast a weary eye back towards the doctors, making sure they couldn't hear. 'Elder Nakobe trusted you, Dev. She trusted you way more than she trusted us. She knew you were going to get good at summoning flember before we did.'

'Hoi!' Bagby protested.

'Oh, it's true,' Pena replied. 'She gave Dev her totem. She wanted Dev to bring us back to Pajoba!' She turned back to Dev, 'It's just . . . while Pockle and Santoro are out there, I . . . I think Elder Nakobe would want you to go and find them.' She smiled hopefully. 'And we . . . we could help too.'

Dev clutched Elder Nakobe's totem in his hand. He stared at the lantern. Slowly, gently, a soft, glowing light billowed up inside it, a light which made both Bagby and Pena grin with delight.

'Well, I did have one idea,' Dev muttered, a smile creeping into his cheeks. He looked across Pajoba, the thin row of huts beyond the trees, then over to dozy, grinning Boja, as all his thoughts slowly merged into one.

'And to do it, I'm going to need the *fieriest* vegetables you have. I don't suppose you grow hibbicus in Pajoba?'

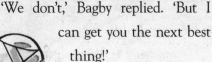

'We don't,' Bagby replied. 'But I can get you the next best thing!'

INVENTION 515: The Paddle Hut

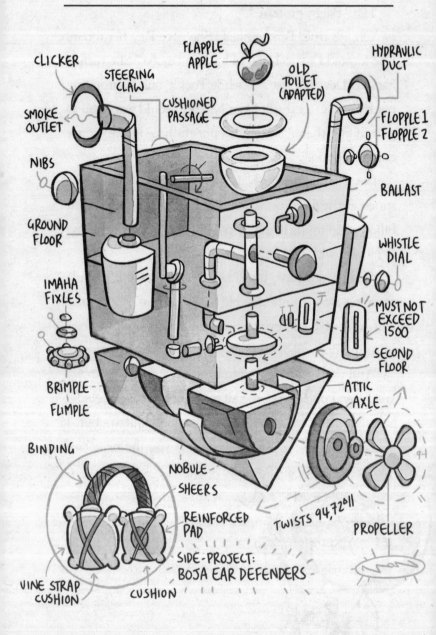

CLICKER

STEERING CLAW

SMOKE OUTLET

NIBS

GROUND FLOOR

IMAHA FIXLES

BRIMPLE FLIMPLE

FLAPPLE APPLE

CUSHIONED PASSAGE

OLD TOILET (ADAPTED)

HYDRAULIC DUCT

FLOPPLE 1
FLOPPLE 2

BALLAST

WHISTLE DIAL

MUST NOT EXCEED 1500

SECOND FLOOR

ATTIC AXLE

TWISTS 94,72°11

PROPELLER

BINDING

NOBULE SHEERS

REINFORCED PAD

SIDE-PROJECT: BOJA EAR DEFENDERS

VINE STRAP CUSHION

CUSHION

27

The Take Off

Dev found a corner of Pajoba in the secluded hills behind the temple where no one would disturb him, and he set to work. There were huts here, huts like the ones he'd found in the camp, only these were square with an extra floor built into each. And, best of all, they were unoccupied. He chose the sturdiest, the one that would need the least sprucing up, fixing, tightening, then had it flipped on to its roof by the big yawning bear with two cushions strapped across his ears.

'FLAPPLE APPLES!' Bagby shouted, dragging a large wooden basket of round fruits up the hill. 'FARTIEST FRUIT IN PAJOBA!'

Stinkbag cantered alongside Bagby, with green gas

prrp-prrp-prrp-ing out behind him. Much to her disgust, Pena was downwind. 'Stinkbag ate a few on the way,' she grimaced, covering Gollup's nose – if indeed it had one – with her cloak.

Dev helped heave the basket towards the upturned hut and Boja, who was sat patiently beside it. 'Now, Boja,' Dev started. 'If you could just—'

He didn't get to finish his sentence. Boja, unable to even hear Dev talking to him in the first place, lifted the basket, tipped it over his head, and dropped a stream of flapple apples down into his open mouth. Then he chewed with all the gleeful relish of someone who hadn't eaten for at least half an hour.

'Deelish-usss!' He beamed, rubbing his belly contentedly.

Dev stared at him in panic.

'You weren't supposed to *eat* them!' he cried, hauling Boja on to his feet. Then he leant all his weight into Boja's big red furry bottom, urging the bear to clamber inside the hut. 'Get in! GET IN QUICKLY!'

'What's all this for?' Bagby asked, chomping a stray flapple apple of his own.

Once Boja had tumbled into the hut, Dev hurriedly pulled himself up behind. He stood in the open space that had once been the hut's living room, but now held

all manner of pipes and dials. 'I call this a Paddle Hut,' he declared, fussing round Boja to get him to sit down on a specially converted toilet seat in the middle of the room. 'It should carry us across the lake. If I can get to the Deadlands first then maybe . . . maybe I can find what I saw of the Flember Stream. Maybe I can connect to it, summon it like Elder Nakobe showed me, and draw it above ground. I can give the flember soldiers something to work with while we look for Pockle and Santoro!' His voice quietened. 'Only . . . the elders don't want me to go, they wouldn't want me building this down by the shore, so I had to think of a way to get to the water from here.'

Strange BOILK noises started to bubble inside Boja's stomach.

Dev let out a yelp, and yanked a belt around his waist.

'Boja was supposed to pour the flapple apples into the engine pipes. I installed around the hut. They were supposed to ferment in there. They would turn into fuel. Into a *propellant*. But now they'll just have to do the same job inside Boja's stomach.'

Bagby and Pena both stared at him in bemusement.

'Boja's going to *fart* us into the sea,' Dev sighed.

'Well why didn't you say? All aboard!' Bagby ran towards the hut, scrambling to climb inside.

'You . . . you can't!' Dev leant over the side. 'I'm sorry, Bagby, Pena, you can't come with me on this one. We're going to the Deadlands. We're going up against the Skraw. It's far too dangerous for you both!'

Bagby stared up forlornly. 'But . . . Pockle's our sister,' he said. 'We have to save her! We HAVE to!'

'Come down,' Pena beckoned to her brother. She lowered her voice to a whisper. 'Dev will find Pockle. You know he will. Elder Nakobe knew he would. We just have to trust in him.'

'BUT . . .'

Pena wasn't arguing. She helped her brother back on to the ground, whispered something else in his ear, then gave him an affectionate hug.

BOILK!

Dev's heart started to race. 'We'll be back before you know it.' He grinned, strapping himself opposite Boja. He looked down to say goodbye, only to see Bagby and Pena had already gone. Only Stinkbag remained, staring back at him, utterly confused by what was going on.

'Well, goodbye, Stinkbag.' Dev waved. 'Maybe *you* can wish us luck.'

'HUP!' Boja suddenly yelped, his eyes bulging larger than ever before as his buttocks unleashed the loudest, most ground-shaking, most fur-ripping PPP-R-R-R-P-P-P-! Dev had ever heard. It billowed down through the pipes, spinning the flopples, the whistledials, blasting through the nobules and then out, launching the Paddle Hut into the air at an *astonishing* speed. Dev didn't even have time to scream. He could barely even see. One minute he and Boja were rocketing up into the sky, and the next they were splashing loudly down into the great lake, quite some considerable distance away from the shore.

Both of them utterly stunned by what had just happened.

Those they'd left behind, the elders, the flember

soldiers, still strapping tree trunks together to try and
make enough rafts, called after them from the shoreline.

But Dev couldn't hear what they were saying. They were too far away. And both his ears had popped.

'It worked!' Dev cried, when he finally got his breath back. He gripped a rather tired and deflated Boja by the paws. 'Somehow, it WORKED!'

Boja smiled politely, looking as if he'd just run five marathons in a row.

'It worked!' came a muffled voice from below. Suddenly, something moved beneath Dev's feet. A bolt. A bolt that held closed a hatch, in what was once the hut's ground floor ceiling. With a scratchy squeak it slid aside. The hatch creaked open. And a few familiar faces poked through.

'It's just like I thought.' Pena grinned, Gollup under her arm, as Bagby helped push her out into the daylight. 'Elder Nakobe trusted you for a *reason*!'

28

Setting Sail

As the torchlights of Pajoba blinked into the distance, the sky, which had been threatening to turn since dawn, finally did. The light grey clouds of morning darkened. A mist drifted across the waters. And although Dev was grateful this was a lake they were sailing on, not the dangerous black waves of the sea, he was still a little concerned by how deep and dark everything looked beneath the Paddle Hut.

'GOLLUP!' Gollup yawned, blinking as it awoke. It cast its glowing eyes around them, smiled sweetly up at Pena, then golluped itself back to sleep.

'GO-L-L-U-P,' Boja yawned. He stretched out his arms, leaning his considerable weight back and causing

216

the other end of the hut to tip up. Soon he was asleep too, snoring, farting and whistling above the lapping waves.

'I'm still not happy about you both coming to the Deadlands,' Dev finally said, as he steered the Paddle Hut through the mist. 'Bagby, Pena. You should have stayed at home.'

'Are you kidding? I finally got away from that stinky wilderpig!' Bagby snorted. 'I mean, he was OK, I suppose. Maybe I was getting used to him. A bit. But anyway, you won't mind us being here when you see what I brought with me!' He reached down into the hatch, and hauled up a tangled, torn mess of leafy robes.

'The Skraw's arm!' Dev gasped, as a cold chill ran through his veins. 'Bagby, if that thing starts playing music again . . .' He looked over at Boja. The Ear Cushions seemed to be tightly strapped on. He hoped, he *hoped*, they would be enough to keep out any noises. 'Well, let's just hope it doesn't.'

'I had my own reasons for

bringing it,' Bagby sniffed. 'When we find the Skraw, I'm going to slap it round the face with this thing.'

Dev carefully took the arm from Bagby. It felt heavy. Sharp in places. He peered at it beneath the gloomy skies, sliding its shredded sleeves back to reveal not flesh underneath, but something far, far more intriguing.

Metal bones.

Pulleys, and dials.

Cogs, screws, bolts and wires, fisplestaws, optylopops, and little flashing lights.

'The Skraw is a *robot*,' he gasped.

'Like Boja?' Pena asked.

'Well . . . a bit like Boja, yes!' Dev muttered, his caution slowly being replaced by an excitement. He gently pressed against one of the claws. A PSCHHHH of steam rolled out from between its knuckles. 'This looks like old technology though, like it's been put together from lots of different parts. Some bits don't fit properly into others.'

Then he noticed the long, metal bone running through the middle of it. It was wrapped with a long white cable, studded with flecks of flemberthyst crystal. It had been pulled taut and rigid, but there was no mistaking where Dev had seen *this* technology before.

'So someone built the Skraw,' he said, staring out across the drizzly grey horizon. 'And I think I can

218

guess who!'

'WHO?' Bagby and Pena asked at once.

'Iola Gray.' Dev scowled. 'We were told about her in Prosperity, how there were three Pioneers who built the city. Grace, who ran the place, my father, who found their flember, *who wrote my flember book*, and then there was Iola Gray. The Third Pioneer. She created their technologies. She built their robots!'

Dev pointed to the cable wrapped inside the Skraw's arm. 'Iola worked out how to put flemberthysts into cables and run flember through them. This must be her work, it *must* be. Who else could build a robot as advanced as the Skraw?'

'HUPPP!' Boja suddenly awoke, his paws clamped over his mouth, as his cheeks ballooned out either side. If such a thing were possible, Dev could have sworn the bear's furry face was turning a little green.

'The waves are picking up,' Dev said, watching the gloomy waters batter against the side of the hut. 'Boja, it's making you seasick. If I can just reach inside your ears, I can recalibrate your balance correctors . . .'

He lifted the Ear Cushions, just a bit, only for Boja to wrench back and swing his head over the side of the hut. Then, with one loud HU-U-U-U-URGHHH the bedraggled bear threw up a stream of flapple apple pulp into the frothing waters below.

'Too late,' Dev sighed.

Suddenly a low, pounding beat started to rattle out around them. It shook through Dev's bones. It shook through the whole hut. Dev turned to see Bagby, wide-eyed and startled, his fingers wedged in between the dials of the Skraw's arm.

'I . . . I was only poking it,' he stammered.

Instantly Boja, his Ear Cushions askew, spun back around. His eyelids flickered. His big red eyebrows rose and sank with the beat. Sometimes together. Sometimes out of sync. His fur started to prickle. A strained growl crept out from between his clenched teeth.

His flember started to crackle along with the rhythm. 'It's not the same music as before,' Dev said. 'But it's still *affecting* him.' He reached for the arm, tugging at the bits he recognized. 'We have to turn it off, we have to turn it off NOW!'

Whatever Dev was twisting only speeded the beat up, which sent Boja's eyebrows dancing to a faster, pounding bass. Other sounds, too, started to entangle themselves. Thin, delicate whines. Guttural moans. Blips, beeps and blops.

It was starting to sound more familiar now.

Dev flung the arm hard against the hut walls and

scrambled towards Boja's Ear Cushions. 'We can't let Boja's flember turn again!' he cried. 'We can't—'

But it was too late. Boja's flember suddenly blazed a bright, angry red, as he let out an almightily loud RO-O-O-O-O-O-O-O-O-OARRRR! Dev shrieked in alarm, his trembling fingers tweaking the arm's dials to their very furthest until CLICK! The frequency of the music flattened out, and suddenly Dev could hear words. Distorted, stretched words.

'Brr-r-rin-gg . . . m-mmee . . . fff-f-f-flem-be-rr-r . . .'

'BRING ME FLEMBER!' Boja boomed, flinging the Ear Cushions off completely. He lurched towards Dev. Dev slid to one side, but Boja's momentum was enough to roll the hut over, dunking his face into the waters. The sharp incline sent Bagby, Pena, Gollup and Dev skidding across the floor, FLOMP-ing them into Boja's big red furry butt. It flipped the bear over, and with a loud SPLASH! he was in the water. Then SPLASH! Bagby followed.

SPLASH! SPLASH! SPLASH! Dev, Pena and Gollup too.

The hut bobbed back up with a CRE-E-E-EAK. And then it started to sink, drifting down into the dark, gloomy depths below. Dev splashed around frantically, gripping on to the Skraw's arm to stay afloat. Its music hissed and fizzed, as the waves eventually crackled it into silence.

And soon the only thing any of them could hear was the whistling of the wind, and the cold, swirling waters around them.

29

An Unlikely Summon

With the music gone, Boja's flember had returned to normal, but he looked weak, exhausted. His fur was sodden. His Ear Cushions had long since sunk into the water. Without anything else to hold on to, Bagby and Pena had clung on to him like a life-raft, but his tired paddling wouldn't keep them afloat for long.

Dev floated beside them. Panic shivered through his body, as he stared up into the wide, misty grey skies. 'I can get us out of this,' he choked, spitting out another mouthful of water. 'There has to be *something* I can do!'

'Can't . . . breathe!' Boja gasped. Dev watched flember sparkling around his arms, sputtering and glitching, trying to form the shape of his flember gauntlets but unable to hold their form. Boja was struggling.

He was *really* struggling.

Gollup crept out from Pena's wet cloaks and slithered up Boja's fur, before resting on top of Boja's head. He was still glowing, but he, too, looked scared. Bagby then crawled close up behind him, gripping on to the back of his sister's cloaks, and hauling her higher out of the water.

'F-f-flember finds a way.' Dev shivered. 'That's what the elders said. Flember *always* finds a way. So we . . . we'll *summon* something to help us!' He grabbed Elder Nakobe's totem as it bobbed past. He held it out towards Bagby and Pena. 'Maybe if we try *together*!'

They both reached out, trembling, holding their own totems against Dev's lantern. He scrunched his eyes closed. He could feel his jaw chattering, his hands shivering uncontrollably. The cold water felt like it was freezing through to his bones. 'Empty your th-th-thoughts,' he chattered. 'Try to k-k-k-keep calm. The elders said that flember always f-f-f-finds a way.'

'W-w-we should summon a D-D-D-Dohan,' Bagby insisted.

Another wave lashed against Boja. This one reached Gollup, knocking the slug clean off Boja's head and sending him splashing down into the water. Pena cried out, but she couldn't reach him, couldn't grab his squishy tendrils in time. Within seconds, the glowing slug was swept underneath.

His glow glimmering into the lonely darkness below.

'NO!' Pena yelled. 'I can't lose you too!'

'Wait! L-L-L-Look!' Bagby's totem was glowing. They were *all* glowing. Not brightly, but enough. Enough to make Dev close his eyes again and try even harder.

'Focus,' he whispered, trying to block all other thoughts from his mind. Thoughts of the wind. The waves. The lashing rain. Of finding Santoro. Of getting home. Of seeing his mum again. Of how they'd fought so hard to even get this far.

Of all the things he still had yet to learn.

'GLUHB!' Boja suddenly gasped, as his mouth sank down below the waves. Bagby and Pena both shrieked and both clung on tighter.

'Flember finds a way!' Dev grimaced, clutching the totem as tightly as he could. His own legs were tiring. He knew Boja couldn't stay afloat much longer. He knew Bagby and Pena were weighing him down.

'We'll find it TOGETHER!'

And then, a light crept in between his eyelids.

A bright light.

Not from the totem, but from the water itself. A huge, beautiful, *shimmering* white light shining below his boots.

A light which was growing, as if it was rising rapidly towards him.

And then suddenly he felt a BOOMP!

Something resembling a huge, squishy, glowing

cushion lifted Dev up and out of the cold water. He looked over to Boja, lying on his back like a beached tuttlefish. Bagby and Pena lay gasping alongside him. All of them as stunned as each other.

Bagby wiped the water from his eyes. 'It's . . .'

'It's GOLLUP!' Pena cried.

'GOLLLLUPPPP!' The belch echoed up into the stormy skies. Not the belch of the small, cute, sleeping Gollup they had carried with them through the Wildening, but the flatulent roar of a HUGE, cute Gollup, way bigger than Boja, way bigger than any creature Dev had ever seen. Its eyes glowed. Its bobbly bits swayed.

Its squishy glowing body sailed gently through the turbulent waves.

'Goh-lllluppp,' Boja mumbled, a contented smile spreading across his face as he rolled over to hug the enormous creature.

'We did it! We found some flember!' Bagby cheered, patting one of Gollup's bobbly bits. 'We summoned it to make Gollup GROW!'

'I . . . I didn't know that was something we could do!' Pena gasped.

Dev rolled on to his back, basking in the spray of the drizzle. He hugged Elder Nakobe's totem close to his chest.

'We had the BEST teacher.' He smiled.

30

An Empty Map

Gollup glided through the waters towards a faint, grey lump of land in the distance. He stopped a little short of the shore, allowing Dev, Boja, Bagby and Pena to splash down into the shallows. The land here looked miserable. Desolate. Huge peaks of sloppy grey mud curled out ahead of them, half hidden behind a low-hanging cloud of drizzle.

Dev's heart sank.

Bagby and Pena were more cheerful, busily patting Gollup in thanks. In turn Gollup smiled a broad, glowing smile, then sank down below the water until only its eyes were above the surface. It golluped out a few bubbles.

'Pockle's going to be amazed when she sees Gollup

all g-g-grown up,' Bagby stuttered, as his teeth started chattering.

'You're still cold,' Dev fussed. 'Quick. Gather round Boja, his flember can help keep us all warm!'

Boja, however, was keeping his distance. He stood a few paces away, bedraggled, dripping wet, staring mournfully at the ground. 'Soh – rrry,' he sighed, a big, aching sigh.

'Boja, it's OK. *You're* OK.' Dev edged closer. 'Your flember, it's not red any more!'

Boja huffed, swaying back and forth on his heels. He was clutching his arm, awkwardly, as if trying to hide something, but Dev could still see what it was. Thin black threads, running from Boja's chest all along the length of his arm.

The red flember had left its poison once again.

Bagby and Pena both cautiously shuffled closer towards the bear. 'It's OK,' Pena said, stroking his damp fur. 'We all know it's not your fault, Boja.'

Boja's flember snaked around them as they shuffled in closer. It lit up their faces. It flushed colour back into their cheeks. They hugged his damp, slightly smelly, fur. And they smiled contentedly.

'At least now we know why the music makes you act so crazy,' Dev said, dragging the Skraw's fizzing arm

across the wet grey mud. 'It was hiding a message at a frequency only you could hear, Boja. It was getting inside your circuitry. The Skraw's music was *telling you* to bring it flember!'

He joined Bagby and Pena beside the big glowing bear. He, too, felt weak. Tired. And while he was sure most of that was from nearly drowning in the lake, he couldn't help but think there was something else. Something aching inside his bones. An uneasy feeling he couldn't put his finger on.

And the worry wasn't helping.

'I hope the doctors get here soon,' he sighed under his breath. 'I don't like that poison being inside Boja.'

Bagby sniffed at the air. 'Well we've *definitely* not been here before,' he said. 'All I can smell is damp fur!'

Pena leant over Boja's damp, furry paw. 'Dev, can we see the map in your book?' she asked. 'Maybe it'll help us find Pockle and Santoro sooner, before the others get here.'

'I'm not sure it'll help.' Dev hauled the flember book from his backpack and placed it carefully on to the ground. Then he arranged the pages in the order he best remembered, and passed the flember-filled F across them, lighting up the lines of the map. Tracing it from Pajoba, across the lake, and on to the final blank page.

'Dad never came this far. So there are no distances, no measurements. It's just a great big nothing.' Dev squinted between the dead trees. 'But I saw the Skraw come from here. I know I did. I saw Pockle. I just . . . I need to work out which way to go.'

Dev closed the book, and stared into the swirling, drizzly mists ahead of him. It looked as if the whole world had been scrubbed from existence. As if he could just take a few more steps and fall off the edge. He stuck Elder Nakobe's totem into the mud. Closed his eyes, and gripped it tightly. He hoped that somehow, *somehow*, even in the desolate plains of the Deadlands, he might be able to summon roots, or silverfish, or anything that could lead the way.

But when he opened his eyes again, nothing was happening.

'Without flember, we're completely lost,' he sighed.

Bagby pulled away from Boja and gestured wildly into the mists. 'Pockle's out there somewhere. You said she was! We can't stop now!'

'Bagby's right, we can't just wait for the elders,' Pena stood alongside her brother and wrapped a supportive arm around his shoulders. 'Whatever we're doing, we have to do it *now*!'

Dev sighed, smearing the tip of his boot through the gooey clay mud. 'Even if we did know which way to go, we can't risk Boja hearing the Skraw's music again! We've already tried mud, leaves and cushions, and none of them worked. There's only one other thing I could do, and I was really hoping I wouldn't have to . . .'

He glanced sheepishly at Bagby and Pena.

'I could try . . . rewiring Boja's brain.'

CLICK!

The noise made Dev look up.

WHIRRR!

He saw Boja clutching the Skraw's arm. His big, red fingers squeezed around its metal bones.

FZZZZZ!

Dev, Bagby and Pena all leapt away from the bear. 'B . . . Boja!' Dev warned. 'Put the arm down. We can't risk it playing any more music . . .'

Boja twisted the arm like it was a twig, rattling it, holding it up to his ear.

A muffled, fizzing sound started to beep-beep-beep out from it.

'BOJA, NO!' Dev shouted.

'Music *calls* me,' Boja huffed, deep in concentration. 'Tells me where to go.'

'What's he doing?' Pena yelled, drawing her bow and aiming a sparkling pink arrow towards Boja. 'Why would he risk turning again?'

'Save Santoro,' Boja mumbled. 'Save Pockle.'

'It's the only way to find the Skraw,' Dev gasped. 'By following its instructions. By bringing it flember! But Boja, it's too dangerous. Any more poison might be too much for your body!'

Boja wrapped both paws around the arm and sque-e-e-eezed it inside his fists. It cracked, and it splintered. Its sounds distorted into one continuous noise. A noise that sank back down through the frequencies and into the pounding, jangling music Dev had so come to fear.

'We'll find another way.' Dev winced. 'You don't need to *do* this!'

Suddenly, Boja stood bolt upright. His flember billowed red, his eyes blazing, his fur standing on end.

He glared down at Dev.

'Bring-g-g-g . . . me-e-e-e . . . flem-m-m-mber,' he snarled.

31

A Dangerous Tune

Before Dev could even react, Boja had picked him up. He let out a RO-O-O-O-O-O-O-OARRR above the music, spun around on his heels and, carrying Dev in one paw and the Skraw's arm in the other, squelched away through the mist. SQUELCH SQUELCH SQUELCH through the mud, CRASH STOMP CRUMPLE across the hollow remains of all the dead tree trunks. Dev bobbed helplessly, his brain rattling around inside his skull. His stomach lurched with every skid. Every slip. Every bounce.

He desperately reached across to the Skraw's arm, but Boja had crumpled it into a bundle of wires and metal bones. And now Dev couldn't see how to turn it off.

THUNK! A pink, fizzing arrow hit the wet ground beside them.

'We'll save you!' Pena yelled as she chased them through the mist. Dev could only just make out her silhouette. Bagby ran behind, struggling to even keep himself upright in the mud.

'NO!' Dev shouted. 'Don't come! You won't keep up, you'll get lost! Stay where you are, at the shore, stay with Gollup. The flember soldiers will be here soon, you have to tell them which direction we went!'

Pena cantered to a halt. 'Are you . . . are you SURE?' she asked.

'PLEASE! STAY!' Dev cried, as Boja hopped between the grey mud dunes, and soon all trace of Pena and Bagby had faded away into the drizzle.

Unable to reach the Skraw's arm, Dev decided to try a different plan. He wedged Nakobe's totem between himself and Boja's palm, he-e-e-aving just enough of a gap that he could slip out. He couldn't just fall to the ground, however. Boja was running faster than a bear should be able to, as the slipping, sliding mud beneath his feet propelled him across huge stretches of the Deadlands as if he was skating across a field of solid custard skin. No, Dev decided to go *up*. He slid the totem between the straps of his backpack, gripped Boja's wet fur and clambered on to the bear's back, climbing up, up, up towards the top of Boja's head.

It took Boja a while to notice.

When he did, he pulled a long, lon-n-n-ng skid, stopping just short of an almost sheer slope down into the lower valleys.

'GRAFSCKKK!' Boja exclaimed, his paws flapping around his head as he tried to grab hold of Dev. 'GRAAA! FTHPTBHH! SPLTBTHBTHHH!'

'Boja, I can't let the music poison you!' Dev cried, swinging out of reach and then up, between Boja's ears. 'But I only have one idea left.'

He sunk his fingers into the fur between Boja's ears. CLUNK! A small panel rose out from the top of Boja's head. Dev saw a spinning circuit of flickering lights

inside. He ran his finger carefully along each one, trying to remember what he had installed, and where.

'Clickets, roval leads, luppynuggets,' he muttered. 'Oh, Boja, it feels like so long ago I built you!'

He jammed his fingers into one of Boja's spinning dials, flicking the spokes, and sending it whizzing in the other direction. The lights around it stuttered, for a moment, as if trying to work out what was going on, before flickering back on in an entirely new sequence.

Boja dropped the Skraw's arm.

He froze.

One of his eyelids flickered.

The music was still playing, yet Boja's flember faded

from red to its usual soft sparkling blue.

'Feel . . . different,' he said, in a voice far higher than either of them were expecting. It surprised him so much he clutched at his mouth as if to stop it coming out. 'I feel . . . I feel . . .' His voice slowly became lower. 'I feeeeeel . . .'

'You might feel a little weird.' Dev slammed the panel closed, before ruffling Boja's fur back into a tuft. 'I changed the frequency in your main circuits. Redialled them so they wouldn't hear the instructions in the music any more.'

Boja blinked roughly thirty-seven times, shook his head, went 'B-B-B-B-B-B-B-B!' then allowed his tongue to drop low out of his mouth.

'I feeeeel . . .' he squeaked, before suddenly all the strength seemed to disappear from his body, and he toppled forwards into the mud with a loud SQUELCH! Dev fell with him, struggling to hold on as Boja's body started to slide in the mud. Slowly at first. But then forwards. Forwards. Over the slight incline of the hill, towards the steep drop below.

'WAKE UP!' Dev cried, clutching Boja's fur as if he were riding an oversized donkey. 'BOJA, WAKE U—'

But it was too late. Gravity had already grabbed a hold of Boja's ridiculously heavy body and started dragging it

down the slope at extraordinary speed. Mud sloshed up around them. Sharp drizzle whipped against them. Dev yelped, shrieked and screamed all the way down until finally, *finally*, they slipped into the gloomy depths of the Deadlands.

The ground started to level.

And Boja, thankfully, SQUE-E-E-E-LCH-ed to a halt.

Dev rolled himself to one side, splatting messily into the mud, before pulling out the totem and using it to drag himself back on to his feet. 'That . . .' he gasped.

'That was not fun for anyone involved!'

He blinked. There was something up ahead of them. Walls. Broken, crumbled walls, poking out from the grey mud. They led towards a shape in the mists. A large shape. A *huge* shape.

'Another temple!' Dev gasped. 'I knew it! The Flember Stream must have reached this far once!'

'THPTHTBHTPHTHHH!' Bubbles rolled out of the mud around Boja's face as he lifted his head, and cast two very tired eyes towards Dev. 'Feel . . . sick,' he moaned. Dev rushed to help the bear sit up, wiping away the sloppy mud from his fur to see a terrifying sight beneath.

The poison was still inside Boja's body.

And it had spread even further than before.

32

The Last Temple

Dev helped Boja to his feet, pulling the slow, sluggish bear towards the temple. If he could just get them inside, if they could just find anything left of the Flember Stream, maybe Dev could help rid Boja of this poison. Maybe he could summon all the flember the soldiers might need to defeat the Skraw.

Maybe he'd even find Iola Gray.

And he could ask her why she had created the monstrous Skraw.

As they walked between the crumbling stone walls, Dev noticed metal parts sticking out from the ground. Robotic arms, heads, little legs half-buried by the wet grey mud. A variety of weird and wonderful little robots,

lying lifeless, silent, as if they'd been trying to escape the temple.

The drizzle chilled against his skin.

'I wonder if they once had flember running through them too,' he whispered. Then a terrifying thought struck him. 'Boja, maybe you should wait out here. Even though the music can't affect you any more, if Iola's inside the temple, if she's been programming robots to steal flember, well . . . you're absolutely *full* of it!'

'HONKKKK!' Boja exclaimed; his circuits had clearly not settled yet. His eyes blinked independently of each other. With some effort he started climbing the temple steps, seemingly quite oblivious to the fact he was now making noises instead of saying words. Dev ran after him, trying several times to make his point.

But all he got was honking in response.

Together, they clambered beneath the large, shadowy archway of the temple. Dev's nerves started to jangle again. He held Elder Nakobe's totem up against the gloom and, to his surprise, its lantern started to glow. It held only the faintest of lights, nothing compared to Boja's crackling flember, but still, it was something.

He'd only taken a few steps, however, when the Skraw's long, pointed beak suddenly loomed out of the darkness ahead of him.

'SKRAW!' Dev shrieked.

Boja let out an alarmed roar, swung himself sleepily around, then threw his full weight against the Skraw. The Skraw crumpled, tumbling from the podium it had been standing on, as the two of them rolled down into pitch-darkness. There came a CRASH! A CRUNCH! A tinkling of broken machinery.

A loud HONK.

A bubbling fart.

Dev carefully navigated down a set of stone steps as Nakobe's totem lit the way. In the darkness he found them. Boja's fists CLANG-CLANG-CLUNK-ed against the Skraw's metal ribcage, denting it, crumpling it, until finally Dev yelled at him to stop.

'It's not moving.' Dev pulled Boja away. 'Look, there's no red glow inside it. No music. No flember. It's like the Skraw is . . . powered down.'

Boja huffed, took one more swipe, then reluctantly stepped back.

Dev lifted his totem to see where they were. Its faint blue glow revealed a huge pile of rubble in front of them. Rocks, boulders, wooden beams, all piled up together in the very middle of the chamber. But it was what ran along the walls that intrigued Dev the most. Row, upon row, of *machines*. Tall ones, squat ones, pokey, bobbly, clunky ones. They had been broken, torn apart, left in various states of disrepair, but still Dev ran his finger across a few of them, scooping a groove into the thick layers of dust.

He wondered what they might ever have been used for.

And then the totem's glow lit up the tapestries hanging above.

They were covered in intricate drawings. Whatever these designs were, they looked beautiful. Dials wired into barpometers, straddled by what appeared to be piplips. A succession of interlocking cogs, all slotted together into what looked, from a distance, like a human body.

'Iola Gray, what *are* you trying to build in here?' Dev whispered under his breath.

There came a loud 'FRUMP!' from behind him. He swung around to see a very tired Boja had chosen one of the machines as a seat, only for his ample bottom to comprehensively crumple it. Bits fizzed and banged around his buttocks.

'SOHHHH-REEEE!' Boja gurned wildly.

'It . . . it's OK.' Dev took a deep breath. 'Whatever these things are for, I don't think anyone's using them any m—'

Suddenly a bright beam of light shone out from underneath the machine Boja was sitting in, casting an image into the air between them. The flickering, glitching image of a person. Despite the pixelly interference, Dev could see a sharp nose. Small, tired eyes. A wide-brimmed hat.

And he realized who it was immediately.

'Iola Gray.' He scowled, carefully passing his hand through the beam of light. The Third Pioneer stuttered

around it. 'She looks like her statue in Prosperity. This must be some kind of . . . of *projection*.'

Boja, still woozy, still utterly exhausted, pulled himself from the machine and reached out towards Iola. He flattened his paw, attempting to pat her on the head. But as his big red fingers slid right through her, fizzling and blurring her image, Boja's eyes widened in fright. He let out a terrified hiccup. Then he cowered, as much as a huge bear can, behind Dev.

Suddenly, Iola's mouth opened.

'I-i-it has been some months since I found this place.' Her voice crackled and echoed through the darkness. She lifted her head and looked up and around her. 'I won't stay here much longer. But it was important that I see it for mys-s-self.'

Then, as suddenly as she had appeared, she was gone.

'No!' Dev cried. 'No, bring her back!'

He turned round and gently pushed Boja back into the buttock-shaped dents in the machine. Something clicked. Then hummed. The machine started to power up again, and suddenly Iola was back in the room.

'. . . edicated myself to my cause. There is still plenty yet to l-l-l-learn,' Iola continued. 'So I record this now as a diary. If the n-n-n-next leg of my journey does not go as planned, then at least some proof of what I have achieved might stay be-be-be . . .'

The image glitched. Iola was gone again.

'Wait, Iola's not even *here*?' Dev folded his arms. 'Then where is she? And where's Pockle? Where's SANTORO?'

Iola's image fizzled back in front of him, causing Dev to jump. Boja had been shuffling his buttocks back and forth in the machine to try and get a good signal, but it was only just holding.

Now, however, Iola's image was slightly further away.

She knelt in the shadows, facing the wall.

'Come he-e-e-ere then.' She appeared to be looking at something out of sight. And then a fizzle of pixels appeared in front of her. They crackled, and glitched, as they struggled to form a shape.

'There y-y-you are!'

The shape moved like a toddler, crawling on all fours before staggering on its feet. Long, thin lines hung from its head, as if tethering it to the wall. It let out a distorted growl. Then it flumped into Iola's arms.

She turned her head, as if she was talking directly to Dev. A proud smile crackled across her face. 'I took B-B-Bartle's work, and I improved upon it. I c-c-c-combined it with my own. I created a *life*.'

'Dad?' Dev gasped, stunned to hear his father's name. 'What does *Dad* have to do with this?'

Iola turned back to the child in front of her, and ran her fingers down to the middle of its chest. 'But it is we-e-e-eak.' she said, suddenly plucking something from between its ribs. 'It-t-t-t is feeble. It needs m-m-m-more gold-d-d-d than I could give it-t-t-t.'

Then she, and the child, fizzled back into darkness.

'I made a mis-sss-take,' her voice echoed out.

A loud bang made Boja jump from the machine as it finally short-circuited around his buttocks. Tired and confused, the big red bear stumbled into the machine opposite, crumpling it, too, under his weight, only to then promptly close his eyes and fall asleep.

A loud, exhausted snore echoed around them.

It was only drowned out by a sudden clanking and whirring from above. Dev looked up to see a cluster of spherical cages dropping down from the higher levels of the temple. Their chains wrenched, dangling them out of reach, but he could still see what was inside.

Animals.

A beaver in one. A fox in another. A long-tailed coyote, a floabafish, a winged stoat, a piggle, a squat-nose

rasslepluck. Each of them wrapped in a nest of glowing cables. Each of them squeaking, and honking, and howling.

'Dev?'

Dev's heart leapt at the sound of his brother's voice. He spotted him in one of the furthest cages, looking as grumpy as ever. Long, glowing cables had been wrapped around his armour.

'Could you . . . could you get us out of these things?'

'SANTORO!' Dev cried. 'What . . . what happened to you?'

'Pockle!' Pockle grinned from the cage beside Santoro.

Her costume of leaves and mud rustled cheerfully, as her own glowing cables lit up her face. 'You found me!' she chuckled.

Suddenly, the cables around both Pockle and Santoro tightened, glowing a little brighter.

'I wish it wouldn't keep doing this.' Santoro winced.

Dev stepped back, watching as a thin blue line of light ran out from Santoro's cage, through Pockle, through the

beaver, the fox, the coyote, the floabafish. 'It's a Flember Ring!' he gasped. 'Like the one I built in Prosperity! It's drawing a little flember from each of you!'

'Feels funny!' Pockle giggled, as if she was being tickled.

'So *this* is why the Skraw needed flember,' Dev whispered under his breath. 'It's using you all like . . . like batteries, like flember *batteries*. But batteries for *what*?'

He watched in fascination as the thin glow of flember traced its way through the cages, along to a bundle of wires to the very middle of the temple, where it hit a cluster of large flemberthyst crystals hanging high above the rubble. It swirled around inside them like a mist, then passed out, along the wires hanging on either side. Once it hit the far wall a network of threads lit up, revealing these walls were not just made of stone, but embedded with metallic parts too. They churned, and hissed, and clanked and clunked as the light passed down, into the corner where Iola had been kneeling and then along, through each and every valley. Between pistons. Between clutches. Between ripple-locked bollop-hinges, each of them stretching and heaving around the beautiful, blue glow.

All the way along to a tiny golden heart embedded into the wall.

Whereupon flember lit the heart.

And two white eyes opened above it.

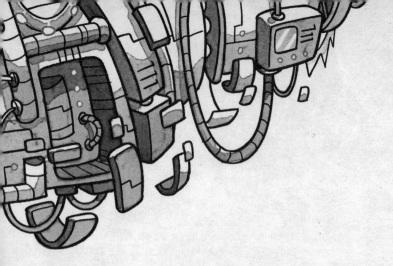

33

Senba

Long stretches of cable slow-w-w-wly heaved the wall
apart, pulling away all manner of robotics that
clunked, and clicked, and slotted together. Its body
emerged like a snake. A huge, thick column of parts,
wires, and animal bones. At its front emerged a face. A
hinged jaw, sharp metal teeth, bristling whiskers. Two
glowing orbs for eyes, above which opened two more
eyes, and then two more. A headdress of pointed, twisted
shards, surrounded by wispy antlers of thin white hair.

And through it all, through all its clacking, whirring,
parts, a faint thread of flember ran between its circuits.

Dev had never, ever seen anything like it.

'SE-NB-A,' it clicked. Its voice was harsh, painful.

Its eyes blinked towards Dev.

Dev tried to hold his nerve. 'Senba? Is that . . . is that your name?'

'Brr-iii-nngg me-e-e flem-m-mber,' Senba's voice started to smooth out, as if whatever dials turning inside its throat were warming up. 'Sen-n-nba ne-e-e-eeds . . . flem-m-mber.'

Dev gulped and took a step closer, as Senba lowered itself towards him. He could hear its breath. It sounded like peas being dropped down a drainpipe. 'It's you, isn't it?' Dev whispered. '*You're* the one sending the Skraw out. *You're* the one commanding it.'

Dev stopped mid-sentence. He stared up at the cages. At Santoro, and Pockle, and all the other animals plucked from the Wildening. At the glowing cables gently drawing at their flember. And then he cast his eyes down to the small golden heart inside Senba's chest. 'You needed their flember . . . to pump through your own heart.'

Dev reached out towards the heart. As he did, an arm emerged from the side of Senba's clattering body, pushing his hand away. Another arm then clunk-clunked above it. Then others, on the far side. Slowly, its whole body rose back up, careful to keep its distance from Dev.

'*You're* what Iola created,' Dev gasped. 'The child we saw. The robot she built to run on flember! But you . . . you got bigger!'

'Left-t-t alone,' Senba gurgled. Its mouth clicked. Trails of rusty spit swung from its jaw. 'Moth-er-r-r left-t-t Senba . . . alone. Thought I w-w-was not alive, b-b-but I was. I was alive. Sen-n-nba hid h-h-heart. Sen-n-nba . . . *rebuilt*.'

'You upgraded yourself!' Dev stood back to take in Senba's full size. Whatever modifications it had made, it appeared to have done so with any random parts it could find, bits of engine, scraps Iola must have left behind, building itself bigger, and bigger, until it not only filled the temple, but now seemed to be embedded into its very walls.

It was immense.

And secretly, to Dev, it was a little impressive.

'But your heart's too small!' Dev sighed. 'It's the only piece of gold inside this whole temple, the only thing that can hold any flember, but it's way too small to hold enough for something as big as you. Even if you took *all* of the flember from this island, you'd still never be able to hold more than a few drops inside your heart.'

'Sen-n-nba wants to li-i-i-ive.'

'Please,' Dev implored. 'Let Santoro go. Let Pockle go.'

'Sen-n-nba needs *flem-ber*.'

'They need their flember too! You can't just *take* it!'

A loud PSCHHH sounded from inside Senba's chest, as its flember-filled gold heart popped out from its casing. Dev could have grabbed it there and then, could have stolen Senba's chance at life, but he hesitated. Before he knew it, one of its arms had reached down and plucked it between two feathery claws, passing it from one arm, to the next, to the next. Over Dev's head, past a weary Boja dozing in his crumpled machine, and towards the rumpled body of the Skraw.

Where it sank the heart down and placed it between the Skraw's ribs.

A gentle blue light shone out from beneath its leafy cloak. Then a sound pulsed through its body. The low, pounding beat of the music. Slowly, the battered creature rose back to its feet, its flember flickering from blue to a blazing red.

As it turned its long beak towards Boja.

And then it pounced.

Boja honked loudly, standing to catch the Skraw between his arms only for the two of them to tumble against the mound of rubble. Somehow the Skraw got behind him, clamping its legs around his waist, its one remaining arm wrapped tightly around his shoulder.

'What are you DOING?' Dev swung back to Senba. 'Call it off! CALL IT OFF!'

Senba, however, was silent. Its eyes were closed. Its entire body paused in mid-air. What little flember once powered through its body was now rushing through the Skraw. Bringing it to life. Controlling it. Boja growled, thrashing around within its grip, trying to slam the Skraw against the walls if only he had the strength to do so. But he was faltering. The black threads of poison were slowing him down. The Skraw's claws only dug in deeper as its tendrils rose up from under its cloak, snaked across Boja's fur, then planted themselves firmly into his chest.

'HWOOO-O-O-OARGH!' Boja roared, as his flember burst out from around him, then spiralled along the tendrils. The Skraw's eyes lit up a bright red, its little golden heart glowing brighter than ever before.

Dev stared frantically around the temple for ideas. His gaze scanning from the lifeless Senba, across Santoro, Pockle and the animals, all swinging gently in their cages, from all the cables and wires strung between them, to the huge chunks of flemberthyst hanging in the middle of it all.

And suddenly, urgently, everything clicked into place.

'I can get you flember!' Dev shouted, holding Nakobe's totem out in front of him. 'SENBA, I CAN GET YOU ALL THE FLEMBER YOU WANT! JUST, PLEASE, LET BOJA GO!'

34

Buried Secrets

The music stopped. The Skraw's tendrils detached. As Boja slumped to the ground, the Skraw fell backwards. Lifeless. Still. All the red glow disappeared from its body, as it released Boja's flember back into him.

Senba's arms lowered and surrounded the Skraw.

One of them plucked the golden heart from its ribs, then passed it along to the other arms. Carrying it across the temple and carefully pressing it back inside Senba's chest.

The heart pulsed with light.

Then its body, too, all the whirring cogs and clicking dials, started to fire back up.

Senba's eyes were glowing once again and its teeth

clack-clack-clacked together.

It breathed out a rattly gasp.

'Sen-n-nba needs flem . . . ber-r-r-r.'

Dev carefully stepped over the Skraw's crumpled body. He knelt down beside Boja. 'Boja, are you OK?' he said, relieved to still feel the warmth of Boja's flember crackling across his fur. 'Did the Skraw hurt you?' Boja mumbled something through pursed lips. His breathing was slow, heavy. His eyes opened and closed. He was not well.

This was not a good place for him to be.

An anger swelled through Dev's veins. He took to his feet, swinging Elder Nakobe's totem towards Senba, about to yell at it for all the pain it was causing.

But then he paused.

Senba was staring back at him. Its long, thread-like whiskers flickered. Its jaw click-click-clicked open and closed. *It's trying to understand*, Dev thought. *No one's explained this to it before. No one's told it this is wrong.*

An arm unfolded out towards Dev, the pointed tip of its claws slowly tapping the end of his nose. 'Y-y-you're al-l-l-live . . .' Senba's voice crackled. 'Y-y-you *live*.'

It beckoned up, towards the cages. To the array of animals the Skraw had plucked out of the Wildening. To Santoro, scowling. To Pockle, waving cheerfully back.

'They-y-y all . . . *live*,' Senba let out a rasping sigh. 'Why can't I-I-I-I?'

Dev held his nerve. 'We were *born* with flember,' he said. 'We're living creatures. Made of flesh. But you were *built*. You were constructed. Iola gave you gold, she gave you flember, but not enough of either. Then she left you alone to figure things out by yourself.'

He lowered Elder Nakobe's totem so its lantern scraped against the floor.

'Well, maybe I can give you a little help.'

He took a few steps, swishing the lantern from side to side as if he was searching for something. 'Dev, no!' Santoro protested from his cage. 'Whatever your plan is, you can't just let this thing have what it *wants*.'

'It wants to feel alive,' Dev called back. 'The least I

271

can do is let it see what that's like! If I can just show how it feels to be connected to the Flember Stream, maybe it will stop stealing living things to find out!'

The light inside the totem glowed slightly brighter.

Dev's eyes lit up.

'Some roots run deeper than others,' he muttered, moving the lantern around as its glow faded, then brightened, then faded again. 'Some roots run deeper than others. Some roots run deeper than others. Elder Nakobe TOLD us what we needed to know!'

Brighter.

Brighter.

Senba loomed alongside him. It watched the light from Nakobe's totem with a fascinated stare. One of its arms reached out, wrapping its claws around the staff. And then, suddenly, it yanked it from Dev's hands.

'WAIT!' Dev shouted. 'I need that!'

'Flemb-b-b-ber,' Senba clicked. Before Dev could do anything, there was a loud CRA-A-A-ACK as the lantern splintered between Senba's claws. The totem crumpled like cheap wood. But what fell out from inside, what plopped down into Dev's open hands, made him gasp in amazement.

A small chunk of flemberthyst crystal.

'Wait! Flemberthyst?' Dev frowned. 'Totems are

just . . . sticks . . . holding a chunk of *flemberthyst*?'

And then it hit him.

'Elder Nakobe wasn't just drawing flember out from the Wildening,' he said, folding his hands around the crystal and squeezing it hard. 'She was drawing it out from *herself*, too! Using the flemberthyst like . . . like a bridge . . . connecting her to the Flember Stream. *That's* how totems work!'

He could feel his strength returning. His tired, aching legs felt sturdy. His mind, clearer. He opened his hands again to see the crystal was glowing brightly now. Not just from his own flember, but from the mound of rubble in the centre of the temple, as the faintest, most delicate wisps of flember trailed towards him.

'The Flember Stream *does* run underneath here,' he said, grinning. 'It's deep, but it's there!'

Santoro leant through the bars of his cage. 'Dev, even if that's true, how are you going to reach it? The Third

Pioneer was here before, and she only had enough flember for one little gold heart.'

Dev clambered up the rubble, stretching himself
up on to tiptoes, until the flemberthyst he was holding
was only a short distance away from the huge, clinking
crystals above. 'Someone put these up here for a reason.'
He smiled. 'But Iola Gray never worked out how to use
them. Iola Gray didn't know how to *summon flember*.'

Then he closed his eyes.

And he cleared his mind.

'But I do.'

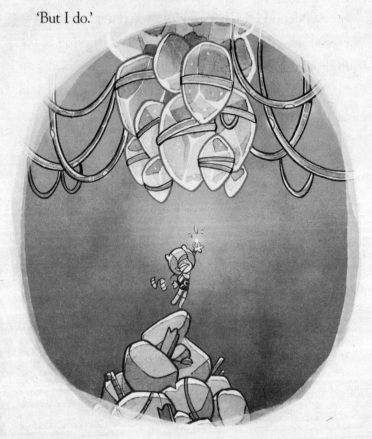

35

Too Much Flember

The rubble started to shake. Thin cracks of light burst out from deep inside of it, spiralling around Dev in wisps, passing through his flemberthyst, then floating up into the hanging crystals above. He could feel it. Could feel the warm, healing power of flember brush against his skin. He crept one eye open to see the smaller rocks start to float up around his boots. Then the larger rocks started to shake. Beams of soft blue light shone out from between them, lighting up the temple. Dev held his ground as long as he could before staggering backwards, tumbling down the rubble as it split apart.

Just as the most dazzling of lights burst through.

It hit the hanging flemberthysts in a thick, shimmering

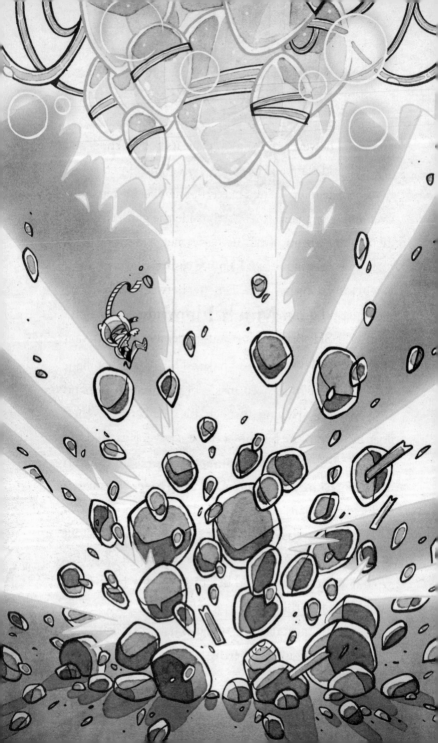

column, lighting them up so brightly they all but disappeared. 'I did it!' Dev cried, shielding his eyes. 'I found the Flember Stream!'

Senba, however, didn't look away. Its body arched, and scraped, and clanked, moving it closer, and closer, to the billowing flember. 'Senba needs f-f-f-flember,' it repeated, over and over again. It reached inside the glow, the scaly metal skin burning from its claws, but it did not seem to care. It was *entranced*. Flember rushed down through its circuitry. Down, inside its body. Between each clanking bolt and turning screw, racing towards the wall and then FOOSH! Bright, blue lines of flember spread along every crevice, every channel, lighting the inside of the temple as if it were a giant glowing circuit.

Senba let out a roar – a deep, distorted roar, which forced Dev's hands over his ears. 'Senba . . . feels . . . *ALIVE!*' it bellowed. Its tattered claws slammed down either side of the Flember Stream. Its whole body wrenched forward from the walls. It leant in closer to the blinding light. And closer. And closer.

'Want . . . more,' Senba snarled. 'Sen-n-nba . . . wants MORE!'

As the temple shook, the cages CLANG-CLANG-CLANG-ed wildly against each other. One cage, holding the piggle, slipped from its rusted bolts and yanked the others a few chain notches down with it. 'This . . . might not have been your best idea!' Santoro yelled, swinging back and forth in the bright light of the Flember Stream.

'I can still see it working!' Dev grinned, leaping across the scattered rubble, reaching up towards the piggle's cage, and hanging his full weight upon it. With an almighty CRE-E-E-EAK it broke free, dragging each cage along the chain with it – CHUNK! CHUNK! CHUNK! – finally bringing Santoro, Pockle and the last few cages down with a crash.

As the animals broke free, fleeing around them in a panic, Dev dragged his brother out from his cage. Santoro gleefully wrenched the glowing cables from around his body. Colour flushed back into his cheeks. His flember armour started to glow. And a scowl returned to his face.

Relieved to see he was OK, Dev then scrambled over to Pockle. She was already clambering out from the remains of her cage, beaming at Dev in delight.

'OK, you found me!' she giggled. 'Now it's your turn to hide!'

Dev unwrapped the cables from around her waist, and he hugged her tightly. 'Let's just get out of here first, OK?' He smiled.

'That's an *excellent* idea!' Santoro yelled, staring nervously up at the ceiling. Senba's metal limbs had been slowly wrenching themselves out from the stonework, straining to get as close as they could to the Flember Stream, and it was weakening the temple. Rocks were starting to fall. The walls were starting to crack. Senba, however, would not stop. As it pulled out, it only grew bigger, dragging at Iola's loose machinery and crumpling new parts of it into its body. Wires, cogs and cables, engines, panels and vents, all threaded and slotted in beneath its metal shell.

It was rebuilding itself.

It was growing.

'SENBA NEEDS M-M-M-M-MORE FLEMBER!' it screamed.

Dev passed Pockle into Santoro's open arms. 'Quick! Take Pockle and follow the other animals out of here,' he yelled. 'I'll wake Boja!'

'I can't leave you. I'm here to *protect* you,' Santoro snapped.

'We'll be right behind!' Dev insisted. 'Santoro, *please*.'

Santoro hesitated for a moment, then nodded, turned and ran, carrying Pockle through the falling dust, and out, towards the daylight.

For Dev, however, waking Boja was easier said than

done. The big red bear was still lying face down on the floor. Still sleeping off his experience with the Skraw. Dev knelt down beside him, whispering urgently into his ear. 'Boja, you need to get up,' he said, eyeing the temple floor as it started to crack around them. 'We can't stay here. We need to get back to Pajoba!'

No response.

'BREAKFAST!' Dev yelled into one of Boja's huge twitching ears. 'REMEMBER HOW BIG THE BREAKFAST WAS IN PAJOBA!'

Boja's eyes popped open.

His whole body sat bolt upright.

A large, rubbery tongue slipped out from his mouth.

'Breakfipple,' he burbled. 'Bribble. Bipple . . . chops. Breakfapple.'

His nose blew a big glowing bubble of snot, as he slowly started to slump again.

'No, no, no,' Dev insisted, heaving the bear upright. 'Boja, if you ever want another Pajoban breakfast, then we have to go NOW!'

Suddenly one of Senba's rebuilt claws came lunging towards them. Boja stood up just in time, staggering out of the way as it embedded itself into the crumbling stone floor behind. He idly scratched his bottom. The bear was sleepy. He was grumpy. But still he begrudgingly stumbled forward, seemingly unaware of what was going on all around him.

'HUNGRY,' Boja huffed, as Dev heaved him up the steep sloping floor. Encouraging him on, towards the temple entrance.

'We'll get you all the breakfast you can eat,' Dev puffed. 'We just need to get out of here . . .'

But as they finally reached the entrance, his heart sank. He looked out at what lay outside the temple.

Sky.

Nothing but sky.

They had walked in this way, but the temple itself had now risen considerably, its lower levels having been dragged up and out of the mud.

'It's lifting the whole *temple*!' Dev cried.

Boja, however, carried on regardless.

Before Dev could warn him, Boja stepped through the doorway and disappeared from sight, bump-bump-bumping down the temple's stone steps. Once he reached the sloped walls previously buried underground he slid on his belly, a-a-a-all the way down to the ground, before landing headfirst, with a loud SQUELCH, into the grey, slimy mud.

Splattering both Santoro and Pockle with great globs of it.

'QUICKLY!' Santoro yelled up towards his brother. 'Do what the bear did!'

Dev gulped, took a deep breath, then threw himself out too. He bounced and flipped down the steps with an OUCH! OOH! ARGH! then flailed down the incline, faster than he might have liked, before slamming into the mud.

'HURGHHH!' he spluttered, barely able to take a breath before Santoro dragged him to his feet and started pulling him away from the temple.

'Run,' Santoro growled. 'Dev, RUN!'

As they scrambled through the slippery mud, huge chunks of rock bounced down around them. Dev turned to see writhing, robotic limbs thrash out through the temple walls, spearing into the ground, heaving the temple along as if it were a giant tortoise shell. Then, with a loud roar, Senba's face broke out through the very top. Its whiskers rattled. Its headdress ruffled. Its jaws clanged open and closed, as its heavily upgraded head leered out across the Deadlands.

'WANT TO LIVE!' it boomed, the bright blue light of flember spilling out all around it. 'SENBA NEEDS MORE F-F-F-FLEMBER!'

36

The End of the Deadlands

As flember washed out from the Flember Stream, spilling across the muddy soil, it drew bright green sprigs of grass from beneath it. Roots crackled and writhed. Stalks plink-plink-plinked up, spiralling, popping into delicate flowers. The animals, now freed from Senba's cages, scattered amongst the newly grown foliage. Life was blossoming, spreading, and as flember hit all the abandoned, half-finished robots, they, too, started to stir. Ocular lenses flickered. Metal fingers squirmed. Cables pulled and antennae beeped, and one by one, they pulled their rusted metal bodies out from the mud.

'I don't understand,' Santoro panted, Pockle clinging to his back as he grabbed on to Dev's wrist and pulled him up the slippery slopes. 'Senba only had a little bit of gold, that tiny heart. That's not nearly enough to lift an entire temple out from the ground.'

Dev reached back to help an exhausted Boja climb up behind him. 'It doesn't need gold at all, not while the Flember Stream is flowing right through the temple,' Dev replied. 'But it won't be able to move *away* from the Flember Stream, not unless . . .'

A thick metal tendril slammed down beside them, knocking Dev sideways. As he skidded to get back on his feet, he saw it burrow down into the fresh grass. Grass which then crinkled and died as its flember pulsed up through the studded crystals of the tendril.

Only for more flember to wash in and grow new sprouts around it.

'Senba's figured it out already,' he gasped. 'As long as the Deadlands keep growing, as long as flember runs through the ground, Senba can just keep taking it. It can carry itself along! It could power itself across the whole island!'

As if summoned, the huge, lumbering shape of the temple rose high above the horizon. It looked like an otherworldly shadow in the mist. Noises bellowed out from inside it. Low, ominous horns sounded. Huge metal limbs hissed and clanked.

'SENBA . . . NEEDS . . . FLEMBER!' it demanded.

Dev gazed at it with a mixture of disbelief and horror. The Third Pioneer had clearly tried to shut her own experiments down, but now Dev had given it what it longed for. He had unleashed it upon Flember Island.

And he wasn't quite sure how he could stop it.

'Keep running!' Santoro grabbed on to Dev's scarf, pulling him across the sloppy mud, while Pockle cheered them both on. Boja lolloped behind, grumbling and mumbling about breakfast until a loud cracking sound drowned him out. The dead tree trunks either side of him were bending and heaving, as dark green leaves started poking out from their flimsy branches. Then the trunks themselves split, as fresh new bark grew out. All the trees around them were growing thicker and taller

than ever before. A forest was growing – a whole *forest* – right before their very eyes.

Dev grabbed Boja's paw and pulled him on, stumbling through the mud as shrubs poked up around them like plumes of smoke. Vines swung down from branches. Huge flowers unfurled across the soft, bouncy grass. Flember spread around and beneath them, the grey, sloppy mud disappearing in a rush of green shoots. As Dev ran, the ground itself seemed to swell, rising like waves, lifting them all up and ferrying them towards the shore at breakneck speed.

'There they are!' Dev suddenly yelled, catching sight of Bagby and Pena by the waters. They waved frantically. Both of them staring, utterly terrified, at the avalanche of Wildening rolling towards them.

'Wh . . . what's happening?' Bagby shrieked.

'POCKLE!' Pena shouted, as Pockle leapt from Santoro's back, and raced across the billowing grass.

'Dev and Boja found me!' Pockle squealed, flinging herself into Pena's arms, only to see the huge, glowing Gollup waiting patiently in the water behind. Her face dropped in total astonishment. She clambered down from Pena's hug, making a noise so excited it sounded as if she was about to burst.

'GOH-H-H-HLUP-P-P!' Gollup cheerfully replied, as Pockle waded into the shallow waters, collapsed into his bright, squishy body, then broke into fits of giggles.

Dev, however, wasn't so excited. 'They're not here yet!' he cried, his heart sinking as he skidded along the shore and stared out across the wide empty lake. 'The flember soldiers, the elders, I was hoping they'd be here to HELP!'

FLUMP! A tree spun out from the ground, leaning lazily over the water. FLUMP! FLUMP FLUMP! A whole line of them, as if they'd been there all along. Boja staggered between them, flopping down against one, trying to catch his breath.

'It's up to us then,' Dev said, tenderly stroking the bear's fur. 'We have to hold Senba back. At least until the elders get here, until the flember soldiers and the doctors get here. We have to take a stand and stop Senba!' He reached into his pocket and pulled out the flemberthyst from Nakobe's totem. 'Bagby, Pena, Pockle, this is what's inside your totems,' he said. 'A flemberthyst crystal. It can carry flember, pull it out from things. It's a conduit. A . . . a tool. What controls it, though, is in here.'

Dev placed his fingers against his heart. 'It's in all of us.'

Bagby stared at him nervously. Then he reached into his cloak, pulled out his totem, and SNAPPED it in half. 'This is what we've been learning to use?' he said, clawing out the flemberthyst crystal. 'A shiny rock?'

'SHINY!' Pockle chuckled, sli-i-i-iding off Gollup and into the shallow waters. Then she pulled her own totem out, handed it to Pena, and watched as she snapped it open.

'It's glowing,' Pockle smiled, holding her flemberthyst up towards the sky.

'It's glowing with your flember,' Dev grinned. 'It's glowing because you believe in it.'

Pena stamped open her own. 'That's great, but what

are we supposed to *do* with them?' she asked.

Dev looked around at the huge swaying trees, the rustling bushes, the thick, dew-soaked grass. 'The Wildening's here now, *flember* is here now,' he said, holding out his flemberthyst.

'So let's use it.'

37

Battle Lines

Dev took a deep breath. He closed his eyes. Clutched the flemberthyst tightly between his hands. He could feel it now. Already. His own flember, swirling around his body, through the flemberthyst, through *all* the flemberthysts. He could feel Bagby standing beside him, Pena, and Pockle, even Santoro as he watched on in bemusement. He could feel the roots glowing beneath his feet, pulling flember up, up through the ground. A flow, back and forth, between them all, a pulsating thread of flember connecting Dev to the island itself.

And then he heard something stirring.

He opened one of his eyes, just a tiny bit, to see a fox snuffling through the newly grown ferns.

A glowing fox.

'We're doing it,' he hissed to Bagby and Pena. 'We're *summoning!*'

'HRGGHHH!' Bagby strained, squeezing his own flemberthyst, clenching his eyes even more tightly closed. From beside him crept strange glowing insects – plonks, mipps, bottle-snops, lesser-buzzing gniplefarps. Then larger creatures emerged. Hedgehogs, each of their spines alight with flember. Glowing weasels. Bagby giggled at the snuffling snout of a flowing bosshog.

'Not quite a Dohan,' Pena playfully teased.

'BETTER than a Dohan,' Bagby snorted back.

Pena focused on her own flemberthyst. It, too, was glowing, flember swirling around it, as the leaves behind her started to rustle. Then slowly, cautiously, a creature stepped out. Its legs were long, spindly, its neck gracefully stretching out as it sniffed the air. Its glow shimmering across the grass.

Pena cautiously opened her eyes, and her face lit up in pure delight.

'A deer!' she cried, struggling to hold herself back from hugging it. 'I did it. I summoned a DEER!'

A growl came from the shore. Dev turned his head just enough to see a small glowing bear splashing through the shallows. It sniffed at Boja's feet, waking him back up, and sending him into contented giggles. 'Keep going,' Dev insisted. 'KEEP SUMMONING!' The bear's mother cautiously followed, a huge, lumbering beast, lit up so bright she looked as though she had crawled out of the moonlight itself. She pulled a glowing fish from the waters, before flumping on to the sands and sharing it with the smaller bear.

Alongside them came a tortoise, a giant, clumsy tortoise, its shell sparkling with light as it stomped casually along the shoreline. Then crabs, skunks, knock-jawed prippets. Dev glanced up, into the trees, to the brightly glowing sloths, jibbermonkeys and large whistlebaboons. And the birds, the bright, glowing birds, singing their hearts out from the very highest branches.

He looked around all the glowing flember animals they had summoned, and he gripped his chest, only now realizing he'd been holding his breath. 'Well then.' He grinned. 'Looks like we have ourselves an *army*.'

A curious, annoying little beep broke through the
beauty of it all. A small robot, not unlike one of those
half-buried by the temple, bumped against Dev's boot.
At first he was tempted to ignore it, until a large metal
stinger curled round from its backside, and tried to jab
him in the leg.

'EUGH!' Dev shrieked, instinctively kicking the robot
away.

'There's MORE!' Santoro warned, drawing his sword.
Sure enough, the hedgerows before them started to rustle,
and a ragtag crew of small robots sped out from beneath.
These, Dev assumed, were Iola's discarded prototypes, the
ones scattered around the temple, temporarily revived by

the Flember Stream
and now scooting, skid-
ding, spinning and rolling towards
the flember animals.

'Absolutely NOT!' Bagby yelled, clocking the nearest robot with the fat end of his hitting stick. He smiled a breathless smile, then swung back for the next.

'We're the children of the Wildening!' Pena declared, drawing her bow, stretching back an arrow, and sending it fizzing between the trees. It impaled another robot into the ground, exploding it in a plume of pink smoke. 'And we'll defend its flember till the end!'

As Dev watched the broken robots racing towards them he noticed something curious. Their flember wasn't blue like the flember spilling across the Deadlands. It was *red*. These robots were being controlled. Instructed. They were being sent to steal more flember.

Just like . . . the *Skraw*!

'It's here,' he gasped, just as an incessant, garbled music pounded up into the skies, and the terrifying, furious shape of the Skraw burst out from between the trees. Its body awash with red flember. Its limbs stumbling, and scrambling, as the dishevelled beast raced across the grass towards them.

'Mine! Honk!' Boja growled, emerging between the trees at the shoreline. Although he was weak, the lines of poison still reaching across his chest, thanks to Dev's attempts to rewire him the music couldn't affect his flember any more.

Boja looked furious.

Determined.

He punched out his flember gauntlets, itching for one last fight with the Skraw.

Only for Dev to step in his way.

'Let *us* try,' he said, closing his eyes, and holding out his flemberthyst. Bagby did the same, and Pena, and Pockle too, all of them focusing their crystals towards the Skraw. All of them believing in the power of their own flember.

'Now,' Dev muttered, as the Skraw's pounding grew louder in his ears. 'Now now now NOW!'

Suddenly a dazzling light spun out from all four flemberthyst crystals. A light so bright Dev could barely look at it. And yet there, just for a split second, he was sure he could see someone standing before them. Someone made of pure light. Of pure flember. Someone who smiled back at them all with one of her wrinkly smiles.

'Elder Nakobe!' Dev gasped.

And then she was gone, lost in a blast of white light that tore through the Skraw in an instant. Its body was shredded, its metal bones scattered, its leaf-covered cloak ripped into dust. Each and every smaller robot shattered along with it. By the time the light had dimmed, and Dev could blink his eyes back open, all that was left was the Skraw's smoking, burnt skull, rolling across the grass.

Dev looked at Pena, Bagby, Pockle and Santoro, none of them quite able to explain what they had just seen.

A terrible howling pulled their attention back. Senba's huge, roaring head rose up from behind the trees, dragging the crumbling temple along behind it. Robotic arms pounded the ground. Tendrils swam out from behind, jabbing into the earth, draining everything of its flember, sucking it all up to illuminate every crack and crevice across Senba's body.

Santoro's armour blazed bright as he pointed his sword out in front of him. Sweat trickled down his cheeks. 'I really wish you'd let me teach you how to fight,' he said, standing protectively in front of his brother.

Dev held his flemberthyst out, flanked by Bagby, Pena, Pockle and Boja with his glowing fists. They in turn were flanked by a dazzling array of flember creatures. A cacophony of stamping hooves. Brays. Snorts. Growls and hollers.

A crackle of flember riding across them all.

'I think we *know* how to fight,' Dev replied, with a glint in his eye.

38

The Last Stand

Dev stepped on to a patch of soft, freshly grown grass, his flemberthyst clutched tightly in his hand. He looked down at the slew of broken robot parts by his feet. Then he lifted his head up towards the huge, hissing, creaking creature looming over them all.

'SENBA!' he shouted up. 'You can't do this! You can't just *TAKE* flember!'

He gulped nervously. Sure, he had . . . *borrowed* a bit of flember himself, back in Eden, to bring Boja to life, but he'd spent all his time since trying to make things right.

'Trust me,' Dev sighed. 'It never ends well.'

Senba let out a distorted roar, sending panicked birds flapping out from the trees. Then it started moving again.

Its arms hissed, and heaved, clawing its huge temple body forwards as it steamrollered a path towards the shore, stopping only a hundred metres short, before slumping back into the ground with an almighty THUDDDDD!

Plumes of dust spewed out around Dev, sending him tumbling backwards. 'Iola should never have done this!' he cried, as Santoro helped him back on to his feet. 'She should never have let you feel what it was to be alive, and then left you all alone. I'm sorry, Senba! That wasn't fair.'

Tendrils lashed out from the temple, puncturing the ground around Dev's boots, and pulling more flember from beneath it. 'S-S-SENBA NEEDS FLEMBER!' Senba gasped, as its face flushed with blue lights.

'That's not how it works!' Santoro shouted, raising his sword above his

head and bringing it sharply through one of the tendrils. Bright, glowing flember spilled and bubbled out. Senba gave a bone-shuddering shriek, as if Santoro had mortally wounded it, then swung a huge arm out towards him. It caught him off guard, clanged hard against his sword, and sent him spinning into one of the trees.

'NEED . . . FLEMBER!' Senba roared.

'Being alive isn't just about flember!' Dev shouted, as more tendrils spun out from around the temple. 'It's about who you are, how you act, how you treat others. It's about how you *live* the life you have!' More tendrils swung out. Dev ducked as one whizzed past his helmet, before wrapping itself around a tree and wre-e-e-enching it out from the ground.

'FLEMBER IS LIFE!' Senba bellowed, grabbing more trees and throwing them as high as it could, as if it were having a tantrum. 'FLEMBER IS EVERYTHING!'

Dev fell to his knees as huge, thick tree trunks smashed down on either side of him. He clenched his eyes shut. Tried to ignore the splinters flying around him, the mud splattering against his cheeks. Tried to focus on one thing only.

The bright, glowing flemberthyst in his hands.

'FLEMBER IS A GIFT!' he yelled over the noise. 'WE'RE LUCKY TO HAVE ANY!'

'A GIFT,' Senba repeated. 'A GIFT. A GIFT. A GI-I-I-I . . .'

Suddenly, all the noises stopped.

The last tree crashed to the ground.

Dev didn't dare open his eyes, but eventually he had to, only to see Senba was now completely still.

Its tendrils hung in mid-air. Its neck stretched out as its six eyes blinked at the glowing flemberthyst in Dev's hands. Just then, the grey clouds above started to break apart. Streams of sunlight shone down upon Senba's face. It tilted its head upwards. Basked in the warmth. Then it looked back down at Dev. At Boja. At Santoro, wobbling back on to his feet, at Bagby, Pena and Pockle. At all the fantastical, glowing creatures lining the shore. They stood like a display of life itself. Humans, next to robot bears, next to all manner of summoned flember animals.

All of them standing in front of one huge, smiling Gollup.

'I have never . . .' Senba started. Its mouth kept moving, but the words broke apart. 'I . . . n-n-never . . . felt th-h-h-he sun. Senba . . . has not . . . s-s-s-seen life . . . like *this*.'

Dev slowly got to his feet. He raised his flemberthyst up as it sparkled in the sunlight. 'Flember brought us all here.' He smiled kindly at Iola Gray's creation. 'That's why we fight so hard to protect it.'

Senba's glowing eyes flickered down towards Dev.

They seemed to be glistening.

'I'm . . . s-s-sorry,' it croaked.

Then, all of a sudden, all the flember drained from Senba's face. From its neck, its metal limbs, from the stone temple itself. Down it flushed, back down into the ground, and as it did, the Wildening around it flourished. Grass grew, shrubs bustled, bushes sprang even bushier than before.

'It's giving it back,' Dev gasped, as Senba's tendrils dropped from the air. 'Whatever powered Senba's heart, it's giving it all back to the Flember Stream!'

Senba's eyes closed shut.

Its mouth dropped open.

And suddenly, Senba was no longer alive.

Instead, it had become like a statue.

39

Heart Surgery

'You . . . did it!' Santoro dropped his sword and wrapped his arms around his brother. 'Dev, you stopped Senba in its tracks!'

Bagby, Pena and Pockle all started hopping excitedly on the spot. 'We *all* did it!' Bagby cheered. 'We kicked that robot temple butt. And we did it by mastering' – he swirled his hands around, as if trying to look mystical – 'flember!'

But Dev couldn't feel quite so excited. 'Senba wanted to know what it meant to be alive,' he sighed, staring up at its lifeless expression. 'It had a right to know. It just . . . went about it the wrong way.'

He slipped his hand inside Boja's big red paw.

'If only it had been given the same chances we gave Boja,' he said.

'Bohhhhh . . .' Boja started, only for his voice to trail off. Suddenly the huge bear toppled backwards, his arms limp, his eyes spinning, his whole body thumping hard into the ground like a barrel of flapple apples.

His bright, sparkling flember started to flicker.

'Boja!' Dev yelled, straining to pull Boja's huge eyelids open. 'Boja, wake up!'

'Bluh-b-buhb-bluhb,' Boja replied, his tongue hanging from his mouth. Dev could see the black threads of poison running through it. He could see the same threads across Boja's fur, from his heart all across his chest, then lacing across one of his arms.

It had clearly spread even further since their run towards the temple.

And now it was taking him over.

'What do we do?' Pena whimpered.

'Flemberthysts!' Dev called, gesturing for each of them to pull out their crystals. 'Hold them over Boja, like this. Summon his flember around his body. This is what the doctors did back in Pajoba, with their totems. This is how they saved him before! Quickly! Santoro, even you!'

'I don't know how . . .' Santoro said, pulling an arm guard from his glowing armour and holding it over Boja as if it might help. But it didn't. Nor did Bagby, Pena and Pockle's summoning skills. Nor Dev desperately begging Boja to open his eyes again. Not even the tender, cautious nudging of the flember animals gathered around them. For whatever flember still remained inside Boja, his body was struggling. His breathing became slower and heavier.

As the poison reached even further through his body.

'There must be something,' Dev muttered frantically under his breath. 'There must be something we can do!'

'We have all the flember we could need around us,' Santoro said. 'And it's still not enough!'

Dev leapt to his feet.

'Of course it's not,' he gasped, clonking his fist against his helmet. 'We're doing it all wrong!'

Without another word, he raced away from the shore, away from Boja and the confused calls of his brother. He ran as fast as he could towards Senba, the fallen temple, and hauled himself up inside its dusty remains. The floor sloped sharply downwards, folded into row upon row of rumpled stone slabs, but still he could carefully slide his way down. He skidded along on the rubble. Clambered over huge metallic arms. Tendrils. Robotic parts wrenched out from the temple walls. Then finally his feet found more solid ground and he stopped, to catch his breath.

The flemberthysts that had once hung from the ceiling now lay smashed on the ground, crumpling the cages underneath. The various machines and control panels had been scattered across the chamber. Huge twisted lengths of cable hung between the walls. They fizzed. And they popped. Sparks showered down across the crumpled floor.

'Perfect.' Dev grinned.

Ten minutes later, he was running back out of the temple, his arms laden with a towering stack of parts. He'd salvaged what he could, what he'd need, a buffet of robotics and mechanics left behind by Iola's half-realized plans. He dumped it all on the sunlit grass, just beside Boja.

Poor, exhausted, rambling Boja.

'Chicken feet,' Boja mumbled. 'Fish bums. Honk honk b-b-blopholes.'

'His flember's fading,' Santoro said, stroking the bear's head with an unusual tenderness. 'And all the flember he was carrying for the Eden tree, too. Dev, whatever your plan is, you need to do it *fast*.'

But Dev had already started. He plugged a few of the loose wires up Boja's nostrils, connecting them to stoppers he then wedged into the bear's ears. Optylopops, fisplestaws, burnt-out fexagons, all connected between half a chunk of engine. 'It's something Elder Nakobe said,' Dev muttered, pounding the engine with the ball of his fist until it PUTT-PUTT-PUTT-ed noisily into action. 'Where there is no light, darkness grows. That's what's happening here. The poison's taking over, instead of the light.'

'But . . . but we tried that!' Bagby insisted. 'We can't get Boja's flember to fight back.'

'Boja's a machine,' Dev said. 'Like Iola made Senba, I made Boja, and I did it the same way – using mechanical parts and a golden heart. But Boja's heart is bigger, more

MODIFICATION: Boja's Flember Kickstart

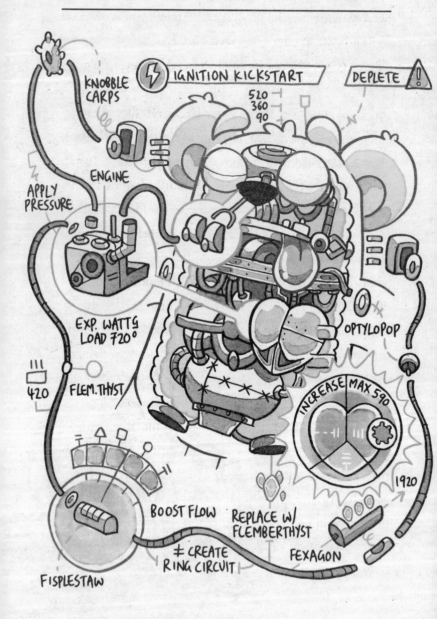

intricately designed. It's more complicated . . .' He pressed the sputtering engine hard against Boja's chest. 'It just needs a bit of a . . . KICKSTART!'

'HOOOOO!' Boja suddenly gasped, his eyes bulging open.

'I've plugged directly into his circuitry!' Dev shouted above the engine noise. 'If we can't move his flember around with flemberthysts, then maybe some good old-fashioned MECHANICS will do it!' He pressed the engine harder against Boja's chest. The PUTT-PUTT-PUTT soon became drowned out by another noise, an even louder noise.

The DOOMPF-DOOMPF-DOOMPF of Boja's heart.

'THAT'S IT!' Dev roared, watching in delight as Boja's flember started to blaze around him. 'Get your heart pumping faster, harder, send all your own flember rushing round your body so fast the poison has nowhere it can hide!'

He looked down at Boja's prickling fur. It was work-ing. The dark black lines were retreating, fading back into the bear's synthetic flesh as they withered against the light. Brighter, he shone. Brighter. And brighter. As his heart pumped faster. And faster. And *faster*!

DOOMPF!

DOOMPF!

DOOMPF DOOMPF DOOMPF DOOMPF!

Dev pulled the engine away. The attachment of cables snapped out from Boja's nose and his ears, whipping across the grass. A crisp, electrifying crackle rode upon the air.

Then an eerie silence fell.

Everyone stared at Boja, at his fizzing, glistening body.

His glow started to settle. His heart started to calm.

As his wide eyes stared out to sea.

And a smile stretched across his mouth.

'Breakfast,' he whispered excitedly.

Dev turned around to see a line of rafts bobbing along the water. At their head rode Pibbles. His raft was heavily laden with what he clearly considered essentials – a huge pile of food, and a towering stack of tables and chairs upon which to serve it all. Behind him, a raft stacked with drums, furiously pounded by a gaggle of drummers. Behind them, a rather frantic looking Elder Pinobei and Elder Knuttle. And behind *them*, a horizon almost filled with flember soldiers.

'You look like you've been busy!' Pibbles exclaimed, staring at the shore in absolute amazement. 'You all must be HUNGRY!'

40

Second Breakfast

Pibbles' raft bumped and bomped alongside Gollup, who GOLLUPed cheerfully. Pibbles marvelled at the remarkable glowing creature, but Pinobei and Knuttle weren't hanging around. They had already spotted Pockle on the shore.

'POCKLE!' they cried, leaping from their rafts and wading frantically through the water. Upon reaching Pockle they squeezed her so tightly it looked like they might never let her go again. Tears streamed down the elders' faces, while Pockle squirmed and giggled between them. Then Bagby and Pena both splashed through the water, piling into the hug.

'We did it! We're flember MASTERS!' Bagby cried,

waving his flemberthyst in the air. Only to drop it, then scrabble around in the water for some time to find it again, before bragging some more. 'We saved the Deadlands with our FLEMBER POWERS!' He beamed at his parents, swishing his arms around for dramatic effect.

Then he froze.

Something was oinking on one of the rafts.

'STINKBAG!' he cried joyfully, rushing through the water and hugging Stinkbag the wilderpig as if they had not seen each other in years. 'Stinkbag, I missed you so much!' Stinkbag oinked and squealed in delight, snuffling Bagby's cheeks and covering his entire face with drool.

Suddenly Bagby realized everyone was looking, and he carefully, sheepishly, lifted Stinkbag on to the shore.

'I mean, hi. I suppose,' he sniffed, blushing a beetroot red. Much to his relief, Pena's deer, her beautiful, glowing deer, wandered over, and stole most of the attention.

'Goodness me.' Pibbles gazed at the deer, skirting round it as if he was scared to get too close. 'You children did this? You did all of this?' He looked over to the glimmering light of flember as it danced between the trees. The brightly glowing bosshogs, weasels and sloths. The hedgehogs, the weasels, the jibbermonkeys and whistlebaboons. The bears and the rhinos. The butterflies, the birds, the buzzing insects flitting between the flowers. He stared up at the huge, towering temple, which looked like it might have fallen from the sky and crashed down in front of them. And then at Senba, poking out from its very peak, its eyes closed. Its tangle of metallic parts shimmering in the sunlight.

And then he caught sight of Dev, Santoro and a flember-filled Boja, standing proudly at its base.

'We did this,' Dev nodded proudly.

'Then we will hurry up and lay the tables,' Pibbles gasped. 'And you must tell me *everything*.'

For the rest of the day, the stretch of land formally known as the Deadlands became a hub of noise and celebration. Or, as Pibbles crowned it, 'second breakfast' (since the first had been so ruined). Drums played. Food was served, and then

gleefully devoured, mostly by Boja. Bagby and Pena ate like the heroes they had become, while Stinkbag feasted on the remains. Pockle, meanwhile, sat on Gollup, merrily handing down bits of food to share.

At the top of the tables, the elders held court, standing occasionally to announce their appreciation to Dev, Santoro and Boja for all they had done.

Glasses were raised.

Bundleturnip wine was sloshed around.

When most of the eating was finished, the latest arrivals from Pajoba stood up from their tables and took a leisurely amble through the lush, bustling foliage of this new Wildening. They petted the flember animals. They smelled the colourful flowers. They stared around in absolute amazement at how beautiful everything looked.

Santoro and Dev remained at the tables. Santoro chomped down on one last picklepork, then let out a long, satisfied groan. 'OK, OK, no more,' he said, wiping a little grease from his chin. 'Now we really ought to get going.'

'You're leaving us?' Pibbles placed a huge bowl of steaming hot jelly stew in front of him. 'But there's still so much the Wildening has to offer. Try this. It's seasoned with poached huffle truffles. They only grow once a year, inside the ears of a ramblemoose.'

Santoro boilked, and pushed the bowl away. 'I . . . I've really had enough,' he whimpered.

Dev picked at the remains of a flonion tart. 'It wasn't your Skraw, Pibbles,' he said, pointing over to the long-beaked skull left lying in the long grass. 'The one we fought. The one we defeated. This wasn't the Skraw carved on the walls of your temple, this was a new one.'

Pibbles plucked a bit of the tart, and popped it into his mouth. 'The word "Skraw" is not really a name,' he said. 'It is a word our ancestors used to describe something that does not respect the rules of flember. It steals flember. It turns flember against those who would protect it. New, or old, this creature was still a *Skraw*.'

'But this is my point,' Dev said. 'This new Skraw came about because Iola Gray was working with flember. Because she was trying to . . . she was trying to . . .' he threw his hands up in exasperation. 'I don't *know* what she was trying to do. But she was an inventor, like me. We don't just . . . *stop* inventing, we don't just give up. Inventing is who we are! So she's probably somewhere else on the island now, still inventing, still experimenting with flember, and that could lead to more Skraws!'

There suddenly came a loud clattering sound, which made Dev jump. He looked over to Pajoba's drummers, who had stepped aside to let Boja gleefully have a go. He'd raised his paw, then brought it down hard, flattening one drum, and sending the others rolling noisily across the shore.

Bagby and Pena cheered. Pockle laughed. Stinkbag oinked.

'Soh-rry.' Boja frowned, before letting out a little oink of his own.

'Hang on,' Santoro said, cramming in a spoonful of hot jelly stew. 'Pibbles, Dev said you were building rafts to come and help us. So how come you loaded them up with food? Surely that slowed you down, when you should have been in a hurry!'

'I told your brother, we believe in flember whatever the odds.' Pibbles tilted his head. He listened to the breeze. 'Aaand someone whispered in my ear that you might be the ones to see this through,' he said.

Dev choked on a tartelette. 'Elder Nakobe? Is she here?'

'She's everywhere,' Pibbles said with a smile, while he brushed a few crumbs from his beard. 'Come on, Dev, you know that by now. Elder Nakobe gave you her totem. Her *totem*. The most precious item an elder of the Wildening can hold, and she gave it to you! She taught you what you would need to know to bring Bagby and Pena home, to defeat the Skraw, to stop . . . this *thing*,' – he waggled a finger towards the temple – 'so you could then save your bear, and bring the Wildening to the Deadlands. Elder Nakobe knew what needed to be done, and who would be the ones to do it.'

Dev glanced at Santoro. Santoro glanced back at Dev. Both of them mid-chew.

'You should both go home.' Pibbles chuckled. 'I'm sure a lot of people are waiting for you there. And hopefully your journey through the Wildening will be easier, now you know a few more of its secrets.'

Dev pulled Nakobe's flemberthyst from his pocket. He rolled it around in his fingers. Then he pressed it against the metal ring of his backpack straps, right in the centre of his chest, until it wedged itself into place.

And it started to glow.

'Thank you,' Dev whispered under his breath. 'And thank you, Pibbles. I've learnt so much.'

Pibbles smiled wistfully. 'It's your father you should be thanking,' he replied. 'After all, he's the one who brought you here in the first place.'

what happened next

Journeys were discussed and plans were made. The people of Pajoba would raft across the lake when their bellies were full and their plates were empty, and the low light of early evening was closing in. Dev, Santoro and Boja would ride Gollup with Pockle, at her personal request. Bagby, Pena and Stinkbag would be joining them. Once loaded up with supplies in Pajoba, Dev, Santoro and Boja would then be sent into the Wildening, tailed by a defensive guard of flember soldiers – just as a precaution – to make their way back to the southernmost mountain.

To make their way home.

So Boja could finally, *finally*, bring flember back to the Eden Tree.

The thought of it sent a thrill through Dev's bones. But something was still gnawing away at the back of his mind. And, since the afternoon skies were slowly flushing from orange to pink, and the party was only just starting to wind down, he took himself away for a little space to think.

He found a spot around the other side of the temple, in its shade. He could still hear Santoro showing off his armour to anyone who might be impressed. He could still see Boja chasing Stinkbag round in circles until one, or both, of them fell over a table. But Dev had brought with him some much more interesting things, things he hoped might answer a few of his questions.

Tapestries, torn from the walls inside Senba's temple, and carefully laid out on the ground.

'What were you trying to do, Iola?' Dev whispered, studying the strange drawings in front of him. He couldn't read the writing, even the symbols didn't make sense, but he could recognize shapes. He could recognize some of the parts. 'Was Senba just a failed experiment? Were you trying to build something bigger?'

He squinted a little closer.

'Did you manage it?'

A low growl broke him from his thoughts. He looked up to see movement between the trees. Black, jagged spines. They slinked through the long grass, slipped behind the rocks, then disappeared beneath the shadows.

The mere sight of it sent a cold fear rattling across Dev's skin. 'A dark wolf!' he gasped, slowly staggering to his feet. He turned his head, about to warn the others, about to call for help, when a thought struck him.

'It looks like it's on its own,' he muttered, scanning the surroundings for other wolves. His fingers ran across the flemberthyst in his chest. 'Maybe I could follow it. Take it on. I'm not the same Dev they came for before.'

The flemberthyst started to glow. A strength rippled through Dev's body, a strength that washed away all thought of the scratches on his arm, or how the wolves had made him feel weak before.

A strength that made him feel *invincible*.

'After all, I can summon flember now.' He grinned.

Dev muttered to himself as he crept through the Wildening. 'You're not like the Skraw, are you? You're not robots. But your eyes, your red eyes, someone's controlling your flember too.' He stopped, as the realization suddenly struck him. 'And they've been doing it for a very long time, if your poisoned skin is anything to go by.'

He sneaked forwards a little more. Out from the trees, and on to an outcrop of mossy rocks. The drop below was steep. It fell down into a gentle river. He peered over the edge, looking for any sign of the wolf.

'Who is it?' Dev whispered. 'Who's controlling—'

Suddenly an intense weakness rushed across him. His head spun, his limbs collapsed, and without warning his whole body crumpled over the edge. It slid down, through the moss, into the reeds below. Dev barely had the strength to pull himself out of the water. Could barely focus on the dark, brooding shadow creeping in front of him.

'There you are,' he gasped, grabbing on to his flember-thyst. 'You . . . you can't hurt me any more. I summon . . . I . . . I summon . . .'

The scratches on his arm started to throb. He looked down to see they weren't just scratches any more. They were spreading, slowly, into thick black veins, running all the way down from his shoulder to his wrist.

Just like he'd seen on Boja.

'Poison,' he wheezed, barely able to believe what he was seeing. 'But . . . but how? My flember is *fine*. No one's controlling . . . no one's . . .'

The dark wolf circled around him.

Its red eyes stared at him with a terrifying intensity.

His thoughts started to blur. His words started to slur. Dev could barely keep his head up, could barely see the dark wolf stepping closer, and closer.

You're looking for me.

The voice echoed loud inside Dev's head.

'Who . . . ?' Dev gasped.

Follow the wolf.

Bring the bear.

'Who are y—' Dev started, but the fuzziness was over-taking him. He couldn't keep his eyes open. Couldn't clear his mind. Couldn't even keep himself upright. All he could do was drift away into darkness, as the voice repeated over and over again.

Follow the wolf.

Bring the bear.

Follow the wolf.

Bring the bear.

Follow the wolf.

Bring the bear.

Bring the bear.

Bring the bear.

BRING THE BEAR.